Weatherman

Sol Senate Cycle: Diaspora

by

Caldon Mull

Silver Bark Books

2023

Publisher information

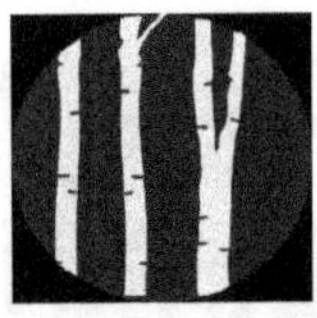

Silver Bark Books
Takapellontie 2 as5
Muurla, 25130
Republic of Finland

Credit section

2nd Edition License Notes

[This page is intentionally blank]

[This page is intentionally blank]

Table of Contents

iv

Prologue

It has started; from a lonely eddy unto a sweeping tide. It started from a single Homeworld sweltering under extreme climate changes and will lead to different places, under alien stars and under strange skies: The Diaspora.

It was early in the first decades of the Twenty-Second Century that whole cities began to enclose their vulnerable population in Arcology structures, protecting them from the chaos and violent weather that swamped whole coastal areas and put paid to the economy of Earth. All the while EarthGov struggled to keep the population of Earth safe on Earth; the more industrious of the Arcology cultures had other plans for themselves. The physical structure of the Arcology culture leaned itself to another type of Enterprise; Travel. In the face of drowning or sinking as an only option, trapped within a ship designed to weather all nature of calamity, humanity became enamored of improving their circumstances in weighting the known and the unknown.

The Ecliptic Emigrant Trail became viable as soon as Arcology technology developed sufficiently within a few decades to optimize the ship systems for Space Flight. Soon enough, City Arcology after City Arcology were lifting off the planet Earth and congregating at Earth LaGrange 5, planning their journey and marshaling their resources to travel the Inter-Planetary Gravity Super-highway.

At the time of this record, ten Earth-flight Fleets have taken to the Ecliptic Trail, and two have taken the longer view to the Seeded Worlds. For the sake of Humanity in the Solar System and the Sol Senate, I have undertaken the task of tracking the experiences of the Human beings in this phase of History that I have classified as 'The Diaspora'.

I make no judgment of these people, I make no claim to vested interests because people are just people. Their tales and experiences are just as valid as any Sol Senator, and add to humanities experience far more reliably than the views that have been passed down through history, based on their views of a privileged few. As in any great endeavor such as this, 'The Diaspora' has to begin somewhere. I have chosen to start close to home with a place that I am familiar with: The Mars-Fleet push from the chaotic Earth. In both literal and figurative meaning, Mars-Fleet had to both establish themselves on a freeze-dried world and defend themselves from the encroaching GovSec.

I hope that these records will be as enlightening to read as they were in compiling.

Excerpts from **'Histories of the Seeded Worlds'** - Titus, **Arktica, 2505AD**

Weatherman

"The drone feeds are in Esteban, you're on in 5…" Esteban nodded, switching over his feed to the news team, waiting for his cue.

"… that was the news and now for the naked weather on Mars, with Esteban Perez…" Esteban grinned with his 'special grin' as the red light on his camera drone flashed 3, 2…

"Thank you, Wasily." Esteban squared his shoulders and picked up smoothly, his internal green-screen display returned his augmented-reality output, along with the other data-tethers to the Skynet satellites. "The cold-front we started tracking yesterday has intensified in the last twenty-four hours to monsoon conditions, indicating heavy sleet and dust conditions along the shores of the northern sink." Esteban ticked off his feed items, "Wally Ramperasadh, you've got about three hours to batten down the hatches and jack your homestead platform up by a meter, it's going to be a long three days before it passes you by and make sure all the stock domes are secured. The trick is to get higher than sixty centimeters, where the dust is most concentrated.

"The rest of you in MF3-Cartagena, after Wally beats down the leading front, keep posted with his manse-com; track what is happening with Wally and the other farmers on the lowland shore. Remember this, if you like lamb chops then Wally and guys like him need to stay safe. If you haven't already, subscribe to the MF3-Cartagena local feeds and keep up to date with the news for your area. Do it soon because you'll probably go off-grid in a day or two.

"On the planetary map, all seems to be just another ordinary day. It's dry and warm out there, all the way around the equator and into the tropics. A typical Martian autumn's day lies in store for us." Esteban concatenated a planetary view in his AR and spun it onto his green-screen.

"Warm fronts around the equator and satellite maintenance above the Hellas lake here in MF1-Cadiz, and in the south polar region are the only change in our twenty-four hour sample and, aside from the monsoon warning, rough weather outside of the domes are *in-fit-tes-imal*." Esteban smiled his 'reassuring smile', "Here are the projections for temperatures and conditions over Mars for the next rotation and for the next week…"

"This is Esteban Perez with the weather for today and for the next week we'll have updates routed through our news team with Babs. I have to go into the shop for maintenance, but I'm back live on the Mars Channel Network in a few days."

Esteban smiled his 'special smile' again holding it as his private feed announced "3… 2… 1… and cut! That's a wrap, people."

"Who else noticed that cell over the Northern sink was going to get so hard, so quickly." Esteban grumbled as he cut his feeds and stomped off his presenter platform. "I thought we had the prediction algorithms down pat. While it's not very deep in the North sink what little water there is, is all going to dump on those homesteads." He growled over at the news platform, Wasily and Babs rolled their eyes in the 'not-this-again' and unclipped their coms.

Lin-ho, the production boss looked over and shook her head "Esteban, it's just the weather… it's not like it's a precise science or anything. Go and put some clothes on, go out and have a beer or something."

"Sure, I'll do that." Esteban grumbled while he headed for his change room, "… just the fucking weather! Right!"

"Chill a bit, the Senatorial parliament feed is back on for the rest of the day, and then Pele Starmind has the rest of the block booked up with his 'Titania – the new Siberia?' documentary. She shrugged, "You've got a whole week before you're on again. Good show… It was a great idea feeding from the homestead's house- mind for the triangulation. We certainly will keep using that, bringing a human face to our viewers."

"Thanks, Boss." Esteban nodded to her as he left the set. "I'm going to get dressed."

Esteban had just tugged on his shirt when there was a tap on his change room door. "Yeah, come in." he muttered, it's not like he was indecent or anything. Martian 'naked weather' was exactly that, and along with his copyright 'special smile' was the fact that he spent his entire working day in the nude. 'What you see is what you get...' as the Mars channel was fond of advertising.

The whole set spent their working hours staring at his junk. Esteban didn't care, and after all this time neither did the rest of the crew. His network contract 'morality clause' didn't prohibit his conduct to any extent as long as he didn't miss a broadcast slot. That was the only thing that mattered to the station, the regular reassurance of the weatherman.

It was Barbara checking in, the channel den mother. "Honey, you okay?" she poked her head past the jam, "I got a weird vibe from you."

"Nah, nothing wrong." Esteban tugged his belt around his hips and shrugged. "Just... y'know... I did all of this stuff so that I could be *important*, but now it seems like I'm just... jewelry... or something. I don't know Babs... I'm fine."

"The next shift is up; we're all going to Yun's in a few minutes. The franchise still has three days to run for the team. You coming?"

"Sure, of course." Esteban shrugged. "As usual, I'm there. We can't have our sponsors disappointed whoever they are. Why not."

"See you there… Just don't order the shrimp again, if you can't eat it… not like last week. You are important to those people out there, Esteban. They could lose everything in a matter of hours if you didn't warn them." Babs' face disappeared and the door clicked shut before Esteban could remind her he didn't *know* he was allergic to Yun's Martian neo-shrimp.

How could he know? Nobody had eaten them before Friday. Not ever. He had *wrecked* that shitter at Yun's; he only left the place after they had closed up. Yun himself had waited for him to limp out the door and begin his trip home. Esteban had burnt those pants as soon as the flux had abated and he finally had the strength to crawl out of his fouled bathtub.

Esteban tugged at his sneaker and his lace snapped. He sighed as he stared at it. 'Recyclable-fashionable-trendy… *fucking junk…*' He scrolled his in-board browser and ordered another to be delivered to his room and it noted that he would be six minutes behind the others arriving at Yun's.

He broadcast an update and waited for the delivery drone to deliver his sponsor's specially crafted size-23 prototype replacement shoelace. "Just great…" Esteban muttered under his breath.

Yun's was pumping as his transport-service dropped him off at the entrance. Inside the establishment he could see Wasily and Babs, Lin-ho and Robert, Natalie from make-up and Roddy from sound engineering, all busy bubbling with the appropriate response to the 'fun' the sponsor wished to project.

They were drawing a crowd and, as Esteban squeezed through the door, they cheered and the waitron-drones flitted above the pack dispensing the house booze as he squeezed through the throng. Esteban smiled his 'special smile' at them and throbbing music started in the background, the lighting changed subtly and a secure-privacy shield shimmer ran up around the space, the after-party was on, baby…

Esteban nursed a water-bottle as the lights flashed and the music throbbed. His augmented metabolism required a relatively enormous amount to stay hydrated. "Mute environment background noise- seventy percent." He instructed his internal browser.

"Ack." It responded as the lights and the noise faded and filtered to his specification.

"Thanks." Esteban sighed.

"Ack" His internal browser responded. It might not have been the best around when he had his modifications done, but it did learn from him, no matter how slowly.

"Hey, big 'un… dat you?" A virtual probe landed at his communications internal staging queue, Esteban immediately recognized the token.

"Hey, hello Pele. Yeah, it's me. What you doing here… aren't you on?"

"Dat de 'ting…" Pele responded in the latest, most fashionable patois, "Mah gonta user ta bestes' ting being virtu-aal… manni place one 'time, yu rule?"

"Sure, I guess." Esteban sighed and steadily sipped his way through his bottle. "I thought you were all the serious newsman now. You know, the 'Martian Canal Network'. MCN this, MCN that… Fuck! You are all over the news… still are… info-tainment…"

Esteban blinked as the data packets streamed into his staging zone, "Fuck it, you don't travel light, do you…?" he dialed up his caching to allow the session more space.

"Yu got da sense of it, but yu gonna 'tink me be un-to-ward by sayin' sumtink gonna be ser-i-yuss downtime, dig?"

"Yeah, me too." Esteban grinned as the famous and fabulous Avatar of the Mars Starmind settled in his internal private virtual forum, "I'll set my private lobby Veep-queue for you, come and join me."

"Mucho 'tanks, mun." Starmind hovered briefly, and then settled with his host, like water on Earth running down a drain. "Yu be still hit da num-bas."

"Yeah, buddy… number two, always number two… to you."

"Big mun, nu-ting wrong wi dat?"

"No, there isn't." Esteban gulped the bottle dry and tossed it into a chute. "I love what I do… it's just that… I don't think they're taking me seriously."

"Wut… you messin'?"

"C'mon even you see just another weatherman."

"Truly. Bes' in buz-i-nuss." The Starmind shell smirked,   "Marriwe, you cy-ba not sof' an' ah no Know-path to maek it gold fo' yu."

"Even if you did, that's not why I'm down." Esteban folded his arms over his chest, the booth seat groaned in protest. "You know me; we've been friends for at least ten years. I wish I had your media credibility. If you were any kind of physical, I'd spread my ass cheeks and beg you to plough me, hoping that some of your inspiration would rub off. But you're not… you're just a collection of data packets visiting my private virtual forum, a ghost in my Veep-queue."

"Heh, Esteban… yu spicy brat-boy." Pele pixilated and pulsed, "I 'spect I could download into a clock an' get you your pan on… metal or flesh, you like?"

"You know I don't care about that shit, Starmind. It is what it is since my frame mods… regular people just can't handle it. I'm getting frustrated with the hand-rubs."

"Yu macho, cathilico, metal-boi… den cy-ba al da ways…"

"You know better than that. Why don't you just call me 'just another stain' and be done with it.

"Esteban…"

"Well, fuck you too, Pele-fucking-Starmind." Esteban blinked, and then growled as his mood swung and the buzz kicked in, "The world isn't like what you present to the public. There are still places on Mars where you can't influence. Not many granted… but there are still places. There's got to be. Some places. Somewhere on Mars… That you can't [hiccup] influence."

"Esteban… [override_Pele-Starmind-shell with Pele-Starmind-core] I'm sorry I appeared offhand with you."

"You aren't speaking newlang V43.2 anymore."

"It's a different Pele_Starmind. You know how I can shell, right Esteban? I know we are more like corridor acquaintances than good friends or anything, but I need your help with something. I'd rather Pele made the contact, I wasn't sure you'd respond to this core persona, the boring Starmind."

"I guess we're all media persona, here. So what's new…? Some personas are real, some are only virtual and most are fake… I'm real, I'm also virtual… I might even be fake. [hiccup] Take Wasily, there… He's a GEN3 from OutSystems. The Mars network has his subscription for two hundred years, he is the 'face of news' until 2430, at least. Him… or any number of identical synthetic human models."

"You're deflecting; Wasily is not what's bothering you." Virtual Pele_Starmind settled into a relaxed pose "What is?"

"No, Wasily is not bothering me. His subscription is not bothering me, that we're the second largest syndicate in the system is not bothering me… Pele… I'm bothering me [hiccup] I'm not feeling it anymore. I've got all the feeds running for coronal activity from the sunspots, I know the quotients, I know what to expect with planetary systems… what to report on… except I don't know what happens with the weather on Luna anymore, I don't know or understand what it does while they're doing [hic] terraforming… it. I mean I do… [hiccup] the physics… but I don't, what it means beyond the Inner system, where they'll [hic] hit [hic] next.

"You're high, aren't you?

"Yup. My sponsor clause is for nine [hic] doses a week. Non-addictive, purely natural high… fresh from the oceans of… [hic] I forget, somewhere off Jupiter. 'Make Mars [hiccup] fun again… with Doctor Indigo…'

"The only side-ef[hic]fect for me is the [hic], is the [hic]…" Esteban grabbed another water bulb and sucked at it, breathing heavily through his nose as he did so.

"Esteban, I can't talk to you like this. I need you to do something for me, and I can't stay long."

"It's my private Veep-queue; it's only open while you're here, Starmind. What do you want exactly? [hiccup] It can't be to hook up, though… if you could get a doll with the right dimensions and attachments [hiccup] download Pele into it, I'm so there…"

"Duly noted. I can't discuss it here." The Starmind pulsed, "The real reason for this veep is that I've got this source and he says there's something in the wind. That it's something you could do. That only *you* should do it. There're no other Pondsmith-05 models on Mars that are available, and I need you."

"I'm bored now Starmind, [hic] make an appointment in my calendar. I'm in for maintenance tomorrow, so I have a few days off for rotation. Talk to me then. I don't think I'd remember anything tomorrow. It's been a long week and I'm cooked right now."

"Sure, Esteban. I'll do that. Starmind out."

Esteban sipped his water while his high peaked and the hiccups faded. Outside the privacy shields' shimmer, Yun's was pumping… lights were flashing with psychedelic intensity beyond his sensory mute settings, people were milling around, jostling, rubbing…

Esteban's erection throbbed and he rubbed it absently. He had a MCN-sanctioned social maintenance appointment and his e-calendar had scheduled his tumescence. Inwardly he groaned as he snapped his phallus free of the constraining fabric, *needing* something a minimum of once a week was not the same as wanting it.

The MCN had requested the alterations when they picked up his contract all those years ago, and they were at least diligent in servicing to specification… a shape pierced the frosted shimmer, right on time.

"Oh hey, I'm Candi… zOMG; it *is* true what they say about you. My friend Mille was your last week; she said you've got an UroQt as well… Everything as advertised… I just can't believe I got your lottery!"

"Yeah, well just rub it, it's not going to fit anywhere in you." Esteban slid down in the booth and angled his hips, "… unless you got synthetics?" he asked hopefully.

"Nope." Candi shook her head, mesmerized. Her hand covered less than half of his girth, "…and it's so hot, like a heating element…"

"I'll keep it at blood temperature for you." Esteban browsed to his internal controls, "Climb on top and get some frottage. You drive it… remember the UroQt is literally a quart, I'll tell you when I'm close."

"Oh, this is going to be so great." Candi wriggled into position against his scalding flesh. I'm going to get me some weatherman rain…"

"It sure is, Candi… sure is… The network appreciates your support…" Esteban pressed the water to his lips as she rode his hips.

Esteban stared out of the window at the dry Martian landscape, dropping his clothes over the hanger.

His hangover pounded in his meat-brain and his abs was still crusty from his 'meet-and-greet' with Candi.

His med-mech company had to be good… you didn't get this high up on the decks unless you were, here on the 114th story. Only the Hegemarch and the Mega-Corporation administration were on the next 16 stories… this was as high as you got in MF1-Cadiz. Esteban wondered which of the Doctors would get to see him today. Partridge was nice, Mukagee was professional, but Waspe was just a self-important snob.

The Hellas Montes Canyon wall loomed directly before him, a few kilometers away from where the Arcology had settled… MF1-Cadiz was 1st Fleet and had touched down on Mars in 2110; while some had flown on to reach Ceres by 2115, others continued on to Jupiter in 2120, all around a century ago.

MF1-Cadiz didn't really have the fuel to continue and they, like MF1-Marseilles and MF1-Sao Paulo and MF1-Bremen were fairly low-status in the 1st Fleet. Landing on Mars was the best they could do.

The 1st Fleet had disbanded in 2120 as was the age old custom, the ships dropping out along the way as they ran the Ecliptic Emigrant Trail.

The Fleet achieved its goal with the last ship reaching its furthest point, for whatever reason; low fuel… ideal landing conditions, a crew or passenger mandate to touch down and end the run on the trail. They were doing well on Mars; it was a good decision in hindsight, for them. Primarily because they got the best spots first, and the Arcology that followed in the 2nd and 3rd Fleets had to adjust to their landing patterns accordingly.

The 2nd Fleet had started from Earth to Luna some decades later, by at least 2140, and had scattered outwards through to Uranus by about 2160, exploiting existing outposts and creating additional ones… ever outwards. The richest and most powerful cities, Shanghai and Osaka were still headed for Triton in the Neptune planetary system, but there was no news of them landing or disbanding the 2nd so far.

Esteban fretted in the geranium-scented room. Nobody seemed sure if the 3rd Fleet could be said to have landed anywhere specific; some had gone to Luna, some had come here… but they *were* welcome where-ever they went… for now; bringing in new tech and updating processes that may have gone stale in isolation, in the hundred-or-so years the 1st Fleet had been out of Earth's influence.

The Earth continued to empty out slowly… one Arcology Mega-Corporation after another admitting defeat on their home world, and following in the footsteps of those who appeared to be more successful. The rally for the 3ʳᵈ Fleet had started on the centennial, and had launched from LaGrange in 2206. Esteban's home Arcology of MF3-Cartagena had touched down on Mars in 2209.

It had drifted in on the rumor mill that the 4ᵗʰ to the 9ᵗʰ Fleets were busy assembling now… running through contracts and terms of engagements… MOU's and MOA's pumping through New Houghton and Arcology after Arcology sniffed around for partners and Fleet candidates… not real news yet, but soon it would be if it were true. Only those GEN Arcology's remained; the synthetic flesh and clone Society.

There was always that dynamic; smaller Arcology linking up with wealthier or more useful ones until the best fit for a successful Fleet, the right set of conditions for a launch into space for the Mega-Corporation Joint Venture that had been formed and agreed.

Still, Esteban couldn't complain… he wouldn't be here otherwise. Here… it was three minutes after his appointment, where was this damned Doctor?

Here, on Mars… MF3-Cartagena would never have been represented in the 3ʳᵈ Fleet if this dynamic hadn't have been the case… it would have drowned on the shores of the Atlantic with all the other buildings that used to be the landed city when the Tides had changed.

At least they had a bit more social cred than MF3-Mumbai. All they had were human bodies, more people than could be safely fitted into an Arcology tagging along, acutely aware of their last place in the Fleet. They had made it, barely, what had happened afterwards was…

"Oh, you're here, Mister Perez." Esteban hadn't met this one before, "I'm Doctor da Silva, and I'll be doing your maintenance this time."

"Please, it's just Esteban." Esteban regarded the tiny woman. "Are you sure you're my med-mech…?"

"Is there a problem?" She regarded him clinically, "You seem distracted, agitated."

"No… of course not." Esteban groaned.

"Good, I don't like it when I get dismissed out of hand. I assure you I'm a fully qualified mech-engineer as much as I am a Doctor. So, you're a Pondsmith-05 Mark-3 commissioned in 2205, before Earthflight."

"Yes, with some modifications and some cosmetics. I didn't really have much choice after the model-05 modifications were completed, my contract was picked up by the MCN and the cosmetics were part of the terms and conditions for them." Esteban shrugged. "The cosmetic mods were added in 2210, when I took up service here in MF1-Cadiz for the Channel."

"At least you're entirely functional… mostly cosmetics just waste my time. You might be my first Pondsmith, but I assure you I'm very good with the mech part of my job."

Esteban grinned, he rather liked Doctor da Silva, "I'm not really utilizing my full functionality though, Doctor. I haven't submerged to specification often enough since I got here. Even the MF3-Cartagena reservoirs are bigger than here."

"1st Fleet or 3rd Fleet design specifications? You look a bit young to be 1st Fleet, early thirties, I'd say. There would be no reason to upgrade to 'archaic' tech" She scrolled through the foil.

"No, almost all 3rd. I had the conversion done on Earth before the last Fleet consignment. I suspect my browser bus might well be 1st Fleet. I spent the trip maintaining the water tanks on the city-ship during the trip. MF3-Cartagena is my home. Every other Sol I am supposed to do inspections and repairs to the cisterns for all the Mars Arcology and their associated World Domes. I've got a tour scheduled this Sol that will keep me busy for about two months after next Easter. My OHSA dicates another diagnostic run before then."

"I'm local here. 4th Generation MF1-Cadiz. Isn't MF3-Cartagena where that monsoon is heading?"

"Yes, since they decommissioned from the Fleet they have other problems. This monsoon is just the least of them." Esteban shrugged.

"Gills?" the Doctor poured through the sections and waved Esteban to a diagnostic slab.

"No, a sterile osmotic skin. It's cleaner and more reliable under intense pressure, you know like sub-crustal oceans."

"The whole skin? The entire organ?"

"Yes, peeled off and completely synthetic. There is an osmotic sub-dermal weave that allows respiration and pressure resistance. I'm good for kilometers down."

"Skeletal Frame?"

"Modifications upgrade to D-Frame... I have a graphene bone-lace. Size makes all the difference on cold submerged missions. To keep my core hot, and to work longer before risking hypothermia, I had to exceed two and a half meters in length. I'm two point seven meters; I put in a minimum tolerance spread."

"Hmmm, that explains your size. How tall were you before the frame?"

"I was one point seventy." Esteban felt a ghost of an ache waft through his bones.

"Must have hurt like a bitch then, that extra meter." She looked up, re-appraising him.

"It did." Esteban sighed; at least his hangover was receding. "But I wanted the Pondsmith; it fit everything I wanted to do out here. It's useful… I'm useful. I want to be useful."

"Sit down there for me and spread-eagle on the diagnosis platform. This is good, high quality sophisticated work. Are you really a meteorologist?"

"Double PhD. Meteorology and Oceanography."

"And the cosmetics…? Surely the penis…"

"The network wanted to project a certain reliable, identifiable image… whether it was in freezing water or out of it. I customized the function of the fluid mechanics they wanted cosmetically, and used that to enhance my heat tolerances. I can transfer and expel heat while submerged and extend my usefulness in hot environments for awhile."

"Still, thirty centimeters by twenty? Mar's most famous organ?"

"It's worth an extra ten degree Celsius tolerance." Esteban squirmed on the diagnosis table.

"Brainwork? What am I dealing with?" The Doctor scrolled through the projections.

"Coms capability, Bluetooth, buffering and cache, low-light optics, onboard camera and sub-vocal broadcast Sonics. Those are all solid 3rd Fleet."

"Echo-location?"

"*Si*, full range of sonar. I have receptor-lines through the skin-weave. Sub-Crustal Oceans are bound to be dark."

"Full-seal system?"

"*Si*. All orifice and meatus included. I can't expel any heated liquids below 300 meters of pressure, so I'm limited in hot environments in a range extent. Cold environments limit me to duration, mostly."

"Impressive, actually impressive." The Doctor snapped the diagnostic panels shut as each displayed green lights.

"Thank you, Doctor. Muckagee doesn't like me much, though." Esteban sat up, towering over the woman.

"He's a purist." She smiled. "He'd object on principle to any contemporary aesthetics. He'd say 'it's a gateway route to fetishism'…" she imitated his voice perfectly.

"*Si*… I'm not sure I like *that* as much as all the other work. It does get messy to maintain. Luckily the MCN has gone out of their way to take responsibility for that."

"The *make him rain* lottery?" Doctor da Silva shrugged, "It seems a bit callous to me."

"It's their property; they can monetize it any way they want." Esteban muttered softly.

"Yes, well… you're completely functional and in good order." She updated Esteban's file, "Your biology is perfect. You've taken an Aquamarine Ooze dose?"

"*Si*, last Sol. It's good for a hundred years, they say."

"That's right. It'll only be wear and tear on your synthetics and cyberware we'll need to check until your dose runs low. Your meat won't even need checking for another sixty years. I should reschedule you for every three Sols, instead of every other one…"

Da Silva blinked into her lens. "That's odd, I've just been booked out by the Starmind… to you, but we're finished here."

"I have no idea what you mean." Esteban shrugged, "I'm offline, like I'm supposed to be during maintenance modes."

"That's exactly right. Just stay on the table, I'll get the booking for the centrifuge." Doctor Da Silva sighed. "This is a priority override. I'll prepare the Mass ooze and the nanites."

"What do you mean? What procedure?"

"How much do you mass, what's your body fat percentage?"

"Two-eighty kilo's and six percent like in the contract." Esteban was puzzled, "What override?"

"I've been instructed to take you to three-ten kilo's and to four percent fat." The Doctor dialed appointments and scheduled materials. "I have to thicken your biological muscle, and there is a lot of it."

"Those are sub-crust ratios for the Pondsmith." Esteban blinked while doing calculations, "That's a six degree or less environment."

"Someone has plans for you, Esteban. I'm just doing what I'm told. It'll be quick, I'll put a protein drip on you after the centrifuge injections, you can go online and hopefully… someone will fill you in. That someone has just bought a week of my time to attend to you."

Esteban sighed. "Sure, whatever… You just tell me what to do, and I'll do it."

"Sorry Esteban, I couldn't wait." The veep connection informed him as soon as he was back online.

Esteban stretched out on a recovery bed, a sonic drip-bit buzzed above his vein; feeding liquids into his system. His back teeth ached as the feedback scratched at his echo-location module, but the Doctor had assured him it wouldn't be very much longer.

It was the only way to complete the procedure, seeing and his skin had a Kevlar-weave as part of his sealed systems rig. Esteban's hangover was only contributing to his discomfort, and he was in a particularly foul mood to boot.

"Starmind… what's going on?" Esteban responded tartly, "What's this about?"

"I really need you to do something for me… on the down low. How are you feeling?"

"A centrifuge really fucks up my Sonics… sick as a dog, actually." Esteban snapped.

"Sorry, I had to do it. I couldn't take a chance that your specifications didn't match, and I have to cover up my actions in case what I'm doing generates unwanted attention."

Esteban relented, "Just don't fuss… it was like this when I got the conversion. I did it before, I can do it again. It's not something I'd do lightly, though."

"That's why I booked the Doctor for you, as your Body Guard." Starmind sounded pre-occupied, "I'm also going to send Pele with you. Hopefully that will cover all the bases. The three of you shouldn't be able to mess things up for me too much."

"You're very kind. So, what next?" Esteban felt a killer case of cotton-mouth starting and reached for a water-bulb.

"There's a transport leaving in an hour from the Flight Bay. I'd like you and the doctor to be on it, Pele will run with the mission."

"My duties with the MCN…" Esteban was beginning to resent the Starmind's attitude.

"…overridden and compensated, there is no contractual conflict at all. You're mine for a week. Remember that I am MCN, I hold your existing contract and the temporary contract you and the Doctor are now seconded to, and any others that I might be inclined to issue."

"Starmind, can you do this?" Esteban felt a creeping dread as to what this was all about.

"Yup, I can." Esteban's Sonics could pick up a brittle note his otherwise flippant remark, "I need a diver and you're the best I've got. I'll send the doctor the Transport Bay number and the departure time. Just you two get there; I'll download Pele_Starmind to a clock and meet you there."

"Starmind, you're really working on my..." Esteban snapped.

"One hour... you'll understand later." Starmind just dropped the call.

"Fucking, fine! Whatever!" Esteban said to no-one in particular.

The drip buzzed and shut down; it dropped from his arm onto a cushion on the recovery couch. Esteban stood and moved to retrieve his clothing when Doctor da Silva walked into the room.

"How do you feel...?" she asked as he stepped into his leggings.

"Like shit, but I'll live. My skin feels really tight, though."

"It's the mass nanites, they've run their course, and the rest of you will catch up in a few hours. Although your skin might look like a normal, perfect summer tan; it really is a semi-rigid mesh. You're actually very tough to treat without specialist mech tools."

"I've heard this all before, the Pondsmith isn't for everyone." Esteban sighed, waiting for his outfit to recalibrate to his new dimensions. "At least I haven't changed a size."

Doctor da Silva watched while Esteban tugged on his boots. "I've just got an address and a time in-mail, but nothing else. Do you know what this is about?"

"Probably no more than you. I ran my eCalendar… and it's true. I've been booked out by an anonymous client for five days… It's the Starmind, that much I know. He wants me to do something and he's been cagey about what it is. Apparently, you're part of the package."

"Starmind? The Mars AI? Pele_Starmind?" she blinked in confusion.

"They might have different Persona… Apparently there is a difference between shells and cores and…" Esteban groaned, his hangover was amplified by the sudden aches in his body as his new muscle fiber pushed against his skin. "…Yup. Same. That one."

"It makes sense, nobody else can afford my rates… so much for so long. It's only that… Esteban, I've been assigned to a 'quantitative asset' and you're a person like me, not a thing."

"Well now Doctor, that's an interesting discussion…" Esteban took tentative steps, trying to balance his new weight, "…that the more money I spend on myself the less free will I have. I don't want to think about that too much, I'd rather not miss that flight. I don't even know where it is going to, but you do. Starmind is keeping the information streams separate. In my personal experience that is never a good thing."

"Compartmentalizing information… mitigates risk." The Doctor shrugged, "I have the mobile toolkit ready for your make and model, we can go anytime you're ready."

"Exactly. Lead on Doctor, we've got fifty minutes until launch."

"Our pod just arrived at the docking bay. I only dialed it five minutes ago. They never arrive this quickly." She tapped the Virtual PA emblem on her smart-sleeve.

"The Mars_Starmind?" Esteban chuckled despite himself, "Our principle contract holder?"

"Oh right, of course. Can you walk, or should I get you an auto-dolly?"

"My knees are wobbly, but otherwise I'm good. I'd lean on you, but then…"

"You'd crush me? Please don't do that," Doctor da Silva smirked, "walk your own damn self."

"Besides which I am a public figure, a hint of anything out of the ordinary will hit the gossip pages and probably work against what Starmind is intending." Esteban tottered behind her and her wheeled mobile, "So Doctor, do you have a first name?"

"While we are on contract, I prefer you just call me Doctor." She quipped over her shoulder, "Just to ensure things remain professional."

Esteban and the Doctor boarded the shuttle in good time. The transport pod arrived for them at the Practice Reception empty of other commuters, stayed empty for a no-stop trip and left equally empty. The shuttle bay-door closed and they strapped themselves into a bank of seats that faced each other over an aisle down the center of the craft.

"There's something up front." The Doctor remarked as she ensured the mobile med-mech kit had locked it's wheels and extended holding magnets onto the shuttle's panels.

"I need to sit for awhile." Esteban muttered, "What is it?"

"It looks like a clock that's busy downloading in the pilot seat."

"That's probably Pele on the way." No matter what he did, Esteban couldn't get comfortable. He thought if he even stubbed his toe, all of his meat would just burst out of his mouth. "Does something look wrong?"

"There's green lights flashing on the controls. I know green lights when I see them."

"Good." Esteban groaned.

"Esteban… why the extra weight? I'm curious, it's a very odd procedure. You mentioned something about six degrees."

"It's an equation for body mass and cold water immersion. The best heat generation is muscle. If you need to spend any time in ultra-cold water, you need muscle mass."

"I'm a medical doctor, what about fat? Why reduce your BMI even further? Doesn't body-fat also provide energy?"

"Sure, energy for awhile… but once it's depleted- and it goes very quickly; it's gone and there are no reserves. You need internal warmth to stay submerged, not energy to move around."

"Fascinating."

"When you're submerged and weightless, you can only move so quickly in that environment, and this movement doesn't require much energy. Warmth, however, is the single significant element for dive duration."

"… and you're a Pondsmith…"

"Yes, these alterations have set me up for my maximum tolerance for the D-frame… somewhere… and taking my base specification as baseline, it's probably an undercooled liquid environment in carbon dioxide permafrost. "

"Are you certain water can stay liquid at those temperatures… ?"

"You would be surprised at what liquid water can do with the right solutes, the right pressures and the right thermoclines. With a medical and technical background I suppose you only see Standard human adaptations to the environment, not necessarily the extremes."

"I suppose so. Cadiz was 1st Fleet and set up in the best environment first. I suppose have got lazy only looking at the range of clients we normally service; mostly cosmetic cyber ware."

Esteban was starting to feel better, his skin discomfort was lessening as the semi-rigid structure conformed to his underlying musculature. His hangover abated, and his Sonic module had successfully rebooted after its whirl in the centrifuge. "Anything from the cockpit?"

"It's not moving, but it looks like it has almost completed the transfer." The Doctor craned forward to peek down the aisle.

"Him… Pele is an alpha, problem solving, goal oriented… ummm. Almost all AI insist on a gender, although I have no idea why. We're nodding acquaintances at MCN. He's a 'he', trust me. This 'Starmind_Pele' Avatar is fascinated with human culture and all that entails. He's done some racy documentaries on human sexuality over the years on the range of preference between mechanical and biological."

"That's interesting, considering how often you appear in the social pages." The Doctor looked over Esteban clinically, "Do you actually have a biological preference?"

"It's all about the sensation for me." Esteban shrugged, "I don't really care about who I share it with, never have…. You?"

"I'm in a Group. I have two wives, two husbands and between us all we have two kids. None of those are mine yet." The Doctor looked down and Esteban had the suspicion there was more to it that that.

"How's that working for you, so far?" Esteban probed.

"It's okay… They treat me right, I get to keep what's mine. I'm an equal among equals. I would probably be more of an equal if I added children into the group…" The Doctor bit her lip and trailed off. Esteban suspected he had hit a nerve.

"Everything a woman in modern society ever needed, now that there are so few around in the 23rd Century. Finally you get equality, but only because you're treated better than everyone else. Treated better as a rare resource." Esteban grinned.

"It's not like that. I'm sure that if I have my own kids, things will settle." The Doctor glared at him.

"Tell me you're not frustrated because nobody is putting you first, treating you like a princess, putting your needs above them… better than an equal…" Esteban smirked at her.

"Esteban," she sighed, realizing he was baiting her, "don't you this start with me. You don't get to solve social issues by slapping me in the middle of them."

"Yeah, I shouldn't." Esteban relented, "I make do, so I guess I'm happy enough. It's not like I have many choices anymore. I shouldn't troll other people about theirs."

"This world is what the World is." The Doctor fidgeted her hands in her lap.

"Somehow I thought Mars would be better with humans on it… I guess I was just foolish to believe that every new place humanity settled would bring a new hope." Esteban grunted.

"Something is moving in the cockpit. I think it's… his… download is complete."

"You folks good back there?" A pleasantly modulated tenor announced itself.

"Hey, Pele. Good enough." Esteban stretched out his legs over the aisle. "You ready to tell us what you're doing?"

"A few more minutes." The synthetic reached for an external USB and slipped it in a port "I just have to set up a false flight to Nuevo Cartagena and dock into an Hotel for us. Then I'll take the controls."

"There's going to be no coms to there soon, for about a week." Esteban shrugged, "What with the monsoon."

"Exactly, that should give us the cover for the time we need. Esteban, you should set your personal location to Cartagena for the next few days and disable it afterwards. Doctor you too. I'll map our departure time to it and bury it in system logs. It should be easy enough to alter our arrival times to it when we're done. The only thing that would notice the difference... is me." Pele smiled with his almost-human clock face, "Or Starmind me... whatever."

"Okay, done." Esteban complied. It felt a bit odd being disconnected, but the contract-holder was the contract-holder, and was always right.

"Make yourselves comfortable as best you can and hydrate a bit, it's about an hour to where we're going."

Esteban was just about getting bored, when the shuttle engine sounds changed pitch and started to bank. The polarized glass cleared as Pele zipped and twisted the four drive pods, finally coming to a stationary hover above what looked like a telescoping dome in the orange landscape.

Esteban could see the far edge of the Planita's horizon covered with the darkness of the GM lily-pads that Mars had so taken to. There must be damp somewhere on the flat plain, or surface ices at least.

"What is this place?" The Doctor pointed at the metal dome.

"It's an old research facility." Pele grunted as he made minor adjustments to the flight stabilizers. "I've put the satellite over it onto maintenance, while we snoop."

Esteban stretched over to the Doctors side of the shuttle and peered through her window. A huge wall of rock stretched kilometers above where the shuttle was hovering in the orange-ish light, a metal marble blinked against the wall a few hundred meters above the scree that lay at the foot of the wall. Pele was inching the shuttle closer and closer to the dome.

They were obviously inside a huge crater... but then again this was Mars, so he still couldn't work out where, exactly.

The dome slid open like a pair of eyelids, a fall of fine Martian dust trailed into the dark cavern it exposed to the light.

Pele banked the shuttle and the hyperwhine of the propellers set Esteban's Sonics on edge. He disabled the mod completely from its 'sleep' state.

"I'll close the dome as soon as we're landed, but the pressure inside is still very low. I wasn't able to activate all of the facilities systems without triggering the system logs." Pele settled the shuttle on the rough geocrete platform.

The Dome slipped closed again until they were sitting in darkness. Red light flicked on in the cavernous bay as Pele shut down the shuttle engines. "Right, we're here." he announced, jauntily settling what looked like aviator mirror-shades over his eyes.

"Where is here, exactly?" Esteban pulled his knees to his chest so that Pele could move down the aisle.

"It's the Argyre, one of the most remote places on Mars... even for Mars. The facility was mothballed by EarthGov about fifty years ago as the Arcology Fleets started to settle. While the Pellas has a micro-climate that is big enough to moderate itself, the Argyre has a micro-climate that is much more extreme, because it is small enough to change rapidly, but just large enough to have a micro-climate." Pele started to open lockers in the racks next to the air-lock. "Doctor, you'll have to get into that SCABU unit in the locker. The air pressure outside here is about twelve percent, just around the Armstrong limit. It's earth-normal in the tunnels, but we have to get there first. There's breathing fluid for you, Esteban... I couldn't find a SCABU suit your size. I checked your specifications back in Cadiz, I'm sure you can make it. I'm purely mechanical, one of the reasons I chose this clock for this mission."

"Its fine, I've done this before. I've got about an hour like this." Esteban guessed it was about a hundred meters to the facility airlock. "When we first made planet-fall, the atmosphere pressure was much less. That was way below my skins' tolerance specifications, no more than about five minutes then."

"I'm sure we don't have another two decades to wait for the atmosphere to reach half a bar." Pele dragged a fluid pump from another locker, "Bring this with you, they didn't have this technology when they built the place and we are going to need to keep this gel aerated for you."

Esteban nodded, "It's only a few minutes to inside, and the pump is light enough." He filled his lungs with the aeration gel while The Doctor suited up, and engaged his Pondsmith control to seal himself completely. He activated his communication module on private short-wave broadcast, "Can everyone hear me?"

"Yes." The Doctor broadcast back.

"You're all good." Pele confirmed, "Come, let's head for the dome. The last one out of the airlock is a rotten egg..."

The clock sealed the cabin door as they gathered in the shuttle airlock and started the sequence. The pressure dropped as the air pumped into the shuttle tanks to match the pressure outside. Esteban felt his skin-weave pinch and pull as it contained his organs against the low pressure environment outside.

It was the same feeling, but the opposite of what he'd experienced underwater in high pressure environments. He supposed it was like the sting you get on a fingertip, except one was with boiling water and the other was with ice... it still stung.

Esteban cradled the gel-pump against his chest and shuffled behind the other two over the geocrete. The Doctor was surprisingly nimble and the two of them reached the airlock well ahead of him. They turned to watch him as his long, but slow strides brought him closer to where they waited.

Frost crusted the clock's cheeks as he started to roll the antiquated door-lock. Esteban's thermometer registered a temperature of minus fifty degrees Celsius in the darkness of the Dome. His smart-suit, while fashionable enough for a visit to the Doctors practice this morning was not happy about its treatment this afternoon. Warning chevrons scrolled over his display sleeve about his immanent wardrobe failure.

The overall-style one piece was icing and shattering in places where environmental moisture from the shuttle was flash-freezing. Esteban himself didn't sweat... couldn't sweat. Perspiration drained on the underside of his synthetic skin to his bladder directly or to his UroQt as overflow.

Esteban sighed to himself as a section of his clothes above one of his knees lost cohesion and sprinkled onto the geocrete in a cloud of minute frozen threads. A patch over his left buttock announced it's disintegration as he stepped over the bulkhead and into the facility airlock.

Pele grinned at him as he spun the door closed and tapped a keyboard near the internal door that lit up when the door registered the seal.

"That was a Pringles." Esteban said on his broadcast, "My favorite suit. You owe me big, clock."

The airlock hissed and started pumping air and Esteban could feel the pinch-and-pull sensation lessening. The sequence ended after about three minutes and the Doctor spun the internal door open.

"What sort of research facility is this?" she asked as they ducked through into a dim corridor.

"It's disused right now, but it is an early EarthGov pioneer facility. It had a military and science squad here about a hundred years ago. They did some core drilling to figure out more about the Martian mantle from here." Pele swiveled the airlock handle and the inner door clicked shut.

"It's also above a subterranean liquid lake. The Argyre was the first landing site to show measurable liquid sub-surface water and volcanic activity as early as the 20th Century, and one of the first identified sites for an outpost. These pressurized tunnels date back very early in

Martian exploration, and they just got bigger and bigger as the activity around them increased.

Until about fifty years ago, when they were mothballed and the staff relocated to the 1st Fleet Arcology that had made planet-fall." Pele motioned for them to follow him down the passages.

"Once they had demonstrated they were successful, no doubt." Esteban muttered. "But that's why I'm here? Liquid water?"

"Pretty much. There is a volcanic plume somewhere far below us that keeps the water liquid, that and pressure… because it's quite deep down there. I needed someone to help me investigate this entire place, even the lake."

"Why are you being so cagey about this?" The Doctor asked, the mobile med-mech in tow; rolling after her, following Pele.

"The facility is officially mothballed, it's in the process of being transferred to Spenser McCormack from EarthGov assets…"

"The boy-genius Terraformer?" Esteban asked.

"The same. Anyway, sometime in the last three years, I noticed this place had a lot of traffic for a mothballed facility, not just the routine mech maintenance RV's, but also people."

"An audit crew? Assizes? Surveyors?" The Doctor asked.

"No… nothing like that." Pele looked down a T-junction, then turned left. "I couldn't find any record in my logs at all. Nothing… something doesn't add up. I've swept the whole base and can't find anything out of place. No people have officially visited here, but the maintenance records show human consumption, for about twenty individuals over this time period."

"How do you figure that?" The Doctor wanted to know.

"The difference between mothballed or disused, and decommissioned is in the supply metrics. The Reactor and the Geo-Thermal installations are maintained in a readiness state, not dismantled and relocated. We might need to reuse any of these facilities at any time, say a Trojan wanders into orbit and the Arcology's are threatened."

"So? It's common knowledge that Mars has old bunkers like these around the Planet." Esteban shrugged. The gel-pump was starting to get heavy, he hoped Pele would stop soon or get to where he was going.

"So hydroponics and oxygen and mess supplies shouldn't need replenishment if there aren't people here to use it."

"… and you're saying there have been here?" The Doctor sounded surprised.

"Yes, about that number of people-visitations over that time. I can't tell if its one person over twenty visits, or twenty people in one visit, or six people and forty mechs in three visits, or…"

"This isn't a monitored facility?" Esteban was curious.

"No, this is too old for that. I've been here before today and swept this place through." Pele stopped before a habitation section and entered a code.

"So why come through today with us?" The Doctor peered inside the quarters as the lights brightened to white in waves to the back of the quarters.

"I haven't looked at the water." Pele motioned them inside. The door shut behind them.

"Ah. So how big is this lake?" Esteban placed the pump down and removed his face-mask to insert the draining tubes down his throat.

"It's big… it's very big for Mars. The logs show that this discovery was the single decision point to go for the planet. By the time this facility was completed, technology had stepped up and it wasn't essential anymore. It's still maintained because of the reasons I've already mentioned; water reservoir, hydro-electric and geo-thermal power that add to the planetary grid but at low reserve levels at present."

"Cold starts to a grid can take years to spin up." Esteban gasped as the last of the gel cleared his lungs and he could breath again. He set the pump to 'aerate' and left the compressor to recharge the fluid.

"Exactly, like this it can be load-sharing within hours." Pele moved to the sections console and began setting environmental conditions while the Doctor stepped out of her SCABU suit and draped it in a hangar-pod. "It's still valuable for additional terraforming initiatives in the collection of resources. The Crater wall here in Argyre is also a fossil crustal fault, where the magma plume is very close to the surface, but I can't confirm this part from the logs."

"This is all stock-standard 22nd Century no-frills military." The Doctor stood in a cabin doorway. "Esteban, you're going to have to lay three of these mattresses on the floor in here. It looks like the sleeping pods top out at two meters."

Esteban glared into the cabin she was looking at, "I wouldn't like to live here. I suppose my only real choice is if I want to sleep with my head next to the shitter, or my feet."

"I think that was the biggest problem with the subterranean habitats here and on Luna and Ceres. You can't really have a civilian population thriving in it. Also, you have about ten kilometers of tunnels and that's it… there is a diminishing return on efficiency after that for ventilation, reticulation and circulation. They fill up very quickly and there's no-where else to go. These are Officer's quarters nearest the command center, the troop dormitories below are quite grim."

"The air smells… odd." Esteban sniffed, "Is the drinking water chlorinated?"

"It must be rock minerals and salts from the water dock." Pele tweaked the environmental consoles, "I'll also increase the CO_2 scrubber's power supplies, it should clear up in a few hours. There are ration-packs in the mess… not as much as there should be, now that I'm looking at the local inventory. Someone else has been here since the last stock count. It's down about fifteen portions from the last count about three weeks ago. That's about thirty five meals in total since I've noticed this first…"

"Martian salts are not the chlorides like on earth, they're perchlorates. They're almost entirely perchlorates… which are toxic to humans." Esteban looked over to the Doctor. "If we're going diving and the salts are a calcium perchlorate, which they usually are, we're going to need to increase our Iodine intake."

"I'm a medical Doctor." The Doctor sniffed dismissively, "Any external activity would require Iodine in substantial quantities. I have anticipated this already. Are there medical facilities near the water dock? If there were military here, I assume they would have appropriate sickbays near appropriate hazard sites."

Pele nodded, "Yes, a pressure sphere and a small ICU facility with triage supplies right near the moon pool."

"Can I get a diagnosis table set up in the space?" she looked at the mobile med-mech and squinted at Pele.

"Ah, nope... they didn't have that tech then and they didn't have patients the size of our boy here." Pele shrugged.

"Great, just great." The Doctor muttered, "I'll have to lay it out here in the common room. What about data facilities in the complex?"

"They're mostly Utilitymind Type-1.5 and Type-2 by our current standards, I'm a Starmind Type-4 that's why I'm here. If you need more 'flops then I'll just veep to my Core."

Pele pointed to data points in the cavern walls, "There's enough communication throughput here, just not terribly complex processors. You had hundreds of horny marines spanking off with their Earth partners when the planets were aligned for broadcast. You needed the throughput if you didn't want a mutiny."

"I guess that will have to do." she sighed. "I'll set up here then for the high-tech stuff and use the facilities as needed. You go on so long while I sort this out."

"We're closest to the Dock in this section, I'll take you to it, follow me." Pele beckoned to Esteban.

They left the section and walked a short distance to an elevator, one which had a single destination button.

"That's simple enough, I suppose." Esteban pressed the button, "Directly from home to work. If only the Arcology were designed like that. Those are real warrens by comparison."

"The advantage of only spending exactly as much effort on what is required." Pele leaned against a wall. "Get comfortable, it's quite a trip."

Esteban discovered he wasn't exaggerating. The speed of the elevator did not seem excessive, but the drop lasted too long for his liking. "How far down is this thing?" he grumbled to Pele.

"About two clicks." Pele didn't seem too perturbed.

When the elevator did finally arrive at the destination, Esteban was actually relieved to get out and stretch his legs. While not exactly claustrophobic, he definitely preferred open spaces above and below him.

The Dock was constructed and sealed away from the lake surface like a blister perched obliquely into a natural cavern space. The tunnel from the elevator lead to a large chamber, with a thick glass wall distinctly separating a dry-dock area from a wet-dock area. Glass cubicles with airlocks further separated the two staging platforms.

"It's all yours." Pele waved a hand at the expanse, "Tell me what you need and I'll look up the inventory for the area."

"I'll need a charge point in the dry area for the gel-pump, I'll need a DPV, a propulsion unit if I'm to cover any ground." Esteban looked around, there was a suitable area next to what was obviously the infirmary.

"There's charge sheds over there." Pele gestured, "They're listed as DPV in the complex asset list. I'm not sure if they've ever been used. They might have collected stuff without having the chance or the focus to use it."

Esteban snorted, "It wasn't common knowledge about how many planets and moons in the Solar System had sub-surface Oceans, or even that Earth has one. They must have only considered this feature as 'component resources'. What's the water like, do you have a chemical composite?"

"It's pure brine. Some of the earliest samples show it to be salt-corrosive, the primary solute is calcium perchlorate as you suspected." Pele blinked as he sped through his internal browser, "I've got no chance if I fall in. This clocks' tin and zinc circuitry won't last more than a few minutes. My aluminum frame will start oxidizing faster than you can spit. I'd keep the Doctor away from the wet-dock without a SCABU suit if I were you. This stuff also scalds skin."

"Not mine. I just have to make sure I've rinsed in a softener before coming through to the dry-dock. The DPV as well."

"The surface temperature is around six degrees Celsius. I'm not sure on any temperature gradients or inversion layers, it doesn't seem there is any survey information on it." Pele grumbled.

"I can handle all that, I'm mostly graphene and some chrome. My skin is organically inert and I can breathe indefinitely through it when submerged. The temperature is a bit of an issue, I can handle up to minus twenty for indefinite periods. I can't handle extreme super cooled water for very long, and there may be layers of it sandwiched under inversion layers, or near dry ice. That shit sticks around minus eighty, and I only have minutes before I'd flash-freeze. I will have to use all the gel for my lungs as a pressure counter-measure to fill all the air-void spaces in my body with liquid if I'm going below three klicks."

"I suppose it's backup oxygen as well, you may as well."

"I can seal all my systems and just use the face-mask. Is there industrial softener-soap for the rinse-showers in your inventory?"

"Yes, they're logged as full."

"Pele, you're the one who has to stay away from the wet dock at all costs." Esteban looked out at the dark, flat water lapping at the moon pool in the other room. "At all costs." he repeated.

"I know. That's why you're here."

"I've tested in the Dead Sea on Earth, this is a doddle by comparison, at least as far as viscosity is concerned."

"Don't get too cocky, Esteban. You don't know what's in there," Pele's head turned to the Bay door, "or what you'll find behind there… or what someone has been doing…"

Esteban tried to quell his excitement, "I think we should eat, get some sleep and start early." He was made for this, his first real chance to do something important.

"Agreed." the clock sauntered back to the elevator, "At least you two should."

▽

"Is everyone in place?" Esteban set the facemask on and broadcast on is narrow band. He set a weight on a long cable with a signal repeater and fed it down the moon pool.

"Yes, we got you." The Doctor's voice came through crystal-clear.

"I'm sealed and going in." Esteban splashed into the pool. "I'll do a pass to get the extent and run my sonar on the passes."

"I'll keep the feeds monitored and the recording from your sensors." Pele buzzed him.

Esteban activated the DPV's strapped to his wrists and sailed into the pitch-dark water. "Fuck this place is big… kilometers wide and at least two deep in most parts." Esteban was literally in his element. He dared not admit this to the Starmind, in case he found more tasks to add to the pot, but Esteban was thrilled to have a chance to do what he was doing now.

He found an inversion layer under about thirty meters that averaged out at twelve degrees and stayed in it. "All conditions nominal" he reported gleefully, at this depth and temperature he could stay submersed for days.

The Doctor confirmed the water was biologically sterile, at least so far. Esteban opened the throttles on his DPV's and coasted on full sonar, just getting a sense of his environment.

"There're some shapes on a rock shelf under the moon pool about three hundred meters down that don't sound geological, I'll go back and have a look after I probe the edge of my coms range."

Esteban used the signal repeater as a beacon. "The water's inversion layers are quite complex, like... a phyllo pastry. There's another warm band at ten degrees one hundred fifty meters below this one, I'll move to that one and scout the lake."

"Noted." Pele sounded bored.

Esteban realized his sense of time had dilated, zigzagging back and forth on full throttle, his sonar cranked up to full, engaging his heat transfer on entering a band of minus three-degree water at four hundred meters; doing a barrel roll around a huge stalactite.

He re-focused and took measure of all of his readings, cruising along and returning to the uppermost warm band, "The lake is shaped a bit like a truncated cone from what my sonar tells me, about seven kilometers wide, maybe about double that where it rests on the mantle, with irregular sides. It might be about forty degrees Celsius down there against the rock, if I would judge from experience of these temperature gradients. It is deep, though… maybe about three kilometers if I figure right. There really isn't much circulation, zero current. It's a completely fossil environment."

"Probably liquefied during the Later Heavy Bombardment and capped by the rock that made the Argyre." Pele speculated. "We have ices above us on the planita, and permafrost for about a klick below the surface, then another click down we have a sealed, fractured and plugged liquid remnant environment. For billions of years there may have been a sea or a glacier above us, completely sealed off from this lake. The Argyre is Mediterranean size at it's biggest extent. Fascinating."

"Your core body temperature has dropped by two degrees going through those cold layers." The Doctor informed him. "But it's stable at this point."

"That's good to hear. It means I have at least another seven hours of bottom time at worst in the cold level. I'm going back to those regular anomalies under the moon pool now. Those reflection readings I picked might be some kind of ore back about an hour on my feeds. It's very dense and reflective to my sonar. Pele, would you check that for me?" Esteban oriented himself cut the speed to half throttle and angled down.

"I'm on it, I'll run the pattern through an XRF spectrometer. My core might have something back in Cadiz."

"I'm picking up organic particulates... They're inert, and they're very faint." The Doctor announced.

"I'm running through some inversion layers on my way down. It's about four degrees on the shelf, just let me narrow my sonar..." Esteban slowed his DPV's to float above the shapes, "*Juipucha?* There are five of them... Its weighted sacks... it sounds like there's something inside the sacks... two arms, two legs a head... they're... human..."

"Esteban, switch on your lights so we can have a look at them." The Doctor prompted, "I can't get a sense of this from your sonic pulses."

Esteban flipped his lamps on in the stygian water and tugged at one of the containers, "*Guacala!*... It's a body, they all are. It's been pickled in the brine." Esteban started at the dead face staring at him out of the sack, dreadfully.

"Open them all, send me the images to identify. Can you bring one up with you?" The Doctor sounded thoughtful.

"They're weighted, but I suppose I can slip one off of the tether." Esteban tugged at the flaps and imaged the pale faces hidden behind the fabric. Once he had exposed all five, he switched off his lamp. He could 'see' perfectly well with his sonar, and he would rather not deal with the corpse 'looking' back at him. In the darkness... it was just a thing.

"Come on up, let's examine the body and see what we're dealing with." Pele made the call.

"I'm on my way." Esteban unhooked the sack and started for the moon-pool. "What are these guys doing here?"

"What are we dealing with?" Esteban stepped from the rinse cycle and threw on a whicking robe and moved into the infirmary where the Doctor was hovering over the corpse he had brought up, dried and put on a dolly for her.

"I've run identification on the images you fed to us, they're all Genetically Engineered Numan Lineages. Specifically two GEN9's, a GEN16, a GEN13 and a GEN6. Four males, one female GEN9. As individuals, there is no real way of identifying them unless you retract their personality chits undamaged... which they are not." she sighed.

"So you're looking at the clone or synthetic Arcology "OutSystems" as opposed to our national "InSystems" Arcology culture." Esteban peered at the corpse, curly thick hair, pleasantly regular features, strong jaw, good muscle.

He could have been any physical age from four months to seventy years old. Most GEN's appeared as young adults irrespective of having just been tanked or at the end of their life-cycle. It had a sunken appearance as the brine had leeched out the body's moisture and a dark mottled scorch mark in the middle of the chest. "Is that the cause of death?"

"Looks like it, pretty much. Electrocution with a massive amperage." she retracted her observation lens. "The sort of injury you'd find on a space ship, where you wouldn't use projectiles or energy weapons."

Esteban was puzzled, "Most of the OutSystems Arcology culture is still based on Earth, isn't it? What are they doing here… I really mean here, at the dark bottom of a Martian subterranean lake?"

"How did they die?" Pele interrupted, stepping through into the infirmary.

"This one has been electrocuted, center mass with a high-amperage slow-slug or prod." she repeated for him, "They still have their personality chits, though… Normally the chips are extracted and re-inserted into the knowledge base, but the amperage used to kill them has also scrambled the data on them."

"So somebody waxed them and dumped them, not knowing enough to extract the chips or destroy them, maybe not aware they have them?"

"Uhhh, not quite. They've been scanned and superficially copied before they've been killed, I can see a broken time-stamp from Ceres in 2224. Who-ever did this wanted these guys far, far away. It looks like they might have died about the same time, with the same weapon. I can only confirm that if I get the others to examine.

Microscopic forensics on the images indicate the GEN6 was the last killed, by maybe ten minutes. Once they went into the brine they'd all have the decay rates suspended at that point."

"Charge weapons run down if used consecutively on that cycle. Maybe there are some broken data packets on the GEN6 that I might be able to retrieve." Pele rubbed his lips, thoughtfully. "Esteban, when can you go and bring the others up? You look like you're out of the water for today."

"I have to de-gas. My cycle should scrub the Nitrogen over the next six hours." Esteban shrugged off the robe. "I can go down again after that."

"Maybe they got careless with the last one. It's a long shot. Enough to kill him but not enough to scramble his chits completely."

Esteban shook his head, puzzled "Wouldn't *anyone* notice if they went missing…?"

Pele shrugged, "I don't know too much about OutSystems society, but if they are mostly interchangeable; then fake credentials, edited personalities, how would you tell…? Superficially the idea is that the members of the society are interchangeable, that the GEN lineages are virtually indistinguishable with each other in OutSystems society. That individuality is less important than societal harmony."

"The medical records indicate that Haroun and Voster created the GEN society to preserve human genetic diversity. So specific recombinant lineages stayed available to the human species. I think the idea was the Sino-6 Inuit cold adaptations, or the Nordic-16 immune systems adaptation wouldn't wash out under environmental pressure and unselective breeding. That distillation of these lineages would be available to enhance the human species... considering how the population numbers of our species have been plummeting." The Doctor draped a sheet over the cadaver. "Human Standard InSystems are augmenting themselves individually to survive, but they intended OutSystems as a buffer against speciation in the long-term to survive."

Esteban sighed, "So what made these five so different? Why are they on Mars if they should still be on Earth?"

"I don't know, Esteban. I can't even guess right now." The Doctor said softly. "Should we leave them here?" she asked of Pele.

"I think so, now that we know about them." Starmind mused, "We can't let the ones who put them here know that we know. At least until we figure out why."

"I've taken GPS readings, I'll drop them in exactly the placing that they were. I didn't move the tether.

 I've got more degassing calculations to do, I can drag them up and take them back down in about ten hours time." Esteban checked his internal indicators "I've also got to rub one out, my UroQt needs attention."

"That's such a stupid augmentation." The Doctor grimaced.

Esteban grinned and stuck out his tongue at her "MCN Marketing thinks its good... think about the sub-conscious affirmation of getting all of this at once," Esteban helicoptered his phallus with a twitch of his hips, "when you're at your most primal..."

"Esteban, you're more than just a hyper-sexualized toy." the clatter of the instruments in the tray she was packing away betrayed her irritation, "You've proved that many times today. You're just being silly."

"Am I? Is anybody, really...?" Esteban's mood changed quickly "Because if not, I'm just a literal ship in a literal desert, doing nothing when I could be doing something. You want me to be useful to you for... I don't know what. Everybody else wants me to be useful to them for this..." Esteban waved his hands over his hips, "... which gets more ratings? One of you or the thousands of them?"

"…" she said nothing, intent of re-packing the med-mech.

"So then, I'm off to go and drain before I clog myself up or trigger the cleaning sequence. It's the 23rd Century, Doctor." Esteban stalked for the elevator.

"Wait up, Esteban." Pele looked up from the console, "I owe you this, and I got the fixtures fitted to this clock before we left Cadiz. The last thing I want is your liquid DNA on all the surfaces here. A promise is a promise."

"Great. What about you, Doctor? You going to join us, or follow me around with a mop?"

"I think I'll stay with this body." She sniffed.

Esteban stretched out on the floor as the clock rolled off his hips. "That's better, thank you." He said drowsily.

"At least you didn't break me." the clock pushed Esteban's feet away from the toilet bowl "What was that about?"

"It's not often I get… y'know, all the way in. I got carried away, it felt good."

"Oh, I hadn't considered that before." Pele pressed a digit into his navel, a metal tube snaked out into the bowl, "A vestigial biological imperative? I don't mind as long as you needed it."

"Thank you for saying so." Esteban yawned "In a way the Doctor is right, I'm crafted to display and for the prospect of sensation; consumed for these things in exchange for increased subscriber ratings and channel loyalty… I am the MCN reward for continued attention from anyone who's interested in them, a sustained drama with a human touch that anybody can sample."

"But you don't like being trivialized like that?" Pele's tube drained Esteban's sexual fluids in spurts, from his augmented cavities.

"Maybe you wouldn't ever understand, Pele." Esteban frowned quickly, "You are a portion of the Starmind, you are actually MCN..."

"Maybe, I would. I'm an AI, crafted to be useful. I always have to ask myself, do I exceed my design by being useful in places other than what I'm designed for?" The clock looked into his eyes, looking for something.

"You're great at human sex, I must say." Esteban yawned, breaking the intense gaze. "I haven't ever had a workout like this."

"A systematic activation of your internal sensory receptors and being mindful of your dulled sense of touch." Pele nodded as the tube retracted and the panel closed seamlessly. "I like to be thorough."

"Do you think we're all just a collection of biological imperative that have been crafted to some short-sighted end?" Esteban murmured softly, drifting off to sleep.

"Now that I wouldn't know about. You'd have to ask a GEN about that." The clock realized he was was talking to nobody. Pele watched the sleeping man for a few seconds, then reached down to kiss him on his forehead and closed the door behind him.

"It's done, they're back." Esteban rinsed off the soap and set the wash-cycle to dry his body. "What's everyone else doing?"

Pele responded "I'm shutting down the facility and returning the logs and states to before we got here. I'll erase the logs remotely once we're underway in the shuttle. I'll also set a drone delivery to replenish our rations on the next supply run on the mothball schedule. That way I can keep track of their activity, and house ours inside theirs."

"I'll just get into the SCABU and then I'm ready. I've reset the Quarters and the living area. Are we heading back to Cadiz, have we changed anything based on what we've found?"

"No, I still think we'll head North, to Cartagena." Pele answered, "Our location settings should confirm once we're back online."

Esteban shut down the shower. "That's where we're supposed to be." He reseated his face mask and did a last check around the dry bay area.

"Correct, our rooms have been booked there for the last two days, we may as well be seen leaving there even if nobody would be able to remember precisely when we checked in." Pele sounded distracted, "Human memory is like that; check in, check out... fuzzy on details in between that."

"I had projected the monsoon hitting today. MF3-Cartagena is on the escarpment, I'm not sure the front had the legs to blow from Tempe Terra up the canyons to Tharsis. It could though, especially if there is more moisture in the swamps that we have been tracking." Esteban retrieved the gel-pump. He may as well drain his lungs on the ship, he still had an hour before it depleted. He cradled it and headed for the elevator.

"We can get in before that uncertainty resolves itself. If we are on lock-down after that, I'll just extend your contract and invoke 'act of god'." Pele assured them.

"It's your money." The Doctor answered.

"Sequence started, shutting the facility down to standby, meet me in the airlock."

"Coming." Esteban acknowledged.

"On my way." The Doctor confirmed.

Esteban wiggled his face mask while Pele spun the hatch. The Doctor stepped out first and made for the shuttle. Esteban dropped the med-mech over the bulkhead lip, retrieved his pump and followed her low-energy hops.

The shuttle airlock hissed open and she moved inside. Being much heavier, he shuffled along the metal platform for the last few meters, while the clock followed after him over the geocrete.

"Why do you think those bodies are here?" She watched Esteban tote the med-mech into the space and place his pump inside bay before pulling his large frame to stand beside her.

"I'm not sure," Pele tapped the keypad as soon as they positioned inside. "If we knew who put them there, we'd get a better chance of knowing why."

The bay equalized and the inner door slid open. Pele made his way to the cockpit as Esteban removed his facemask and reached for the gel apparatus to empty his lungs.

"Do you think it's anything to do with the EarthGov ownership change?"

"It could be." Pele busied himself on the flight console, "It could be a nasty surprise waiting for the new owner… leverage perhaps? EarthGov is not about to sabotage themselves, but it is hardly a unified organization."

"It has to be more than that." Esteban spluttered finally as the tanks registered full extraction. "The "OutSystems" Arcology represent almost all of the manufacturing capability left on Earth. With our 'InSystems' already deployed on Luna, Ceres and Mars, why would you want to cripple them?"

"Maybe you don't want to cripple them… maybe you want to subvert them for yourself." Pele muttered as he deftly worked the controls.

"That sounds reasonable. Far more likely, actually." The Doctor stepped out of her SCABU suit and draped it in its hangar.

"OutSystems are a better option if you're going after Arcology culture. Titus-net and I have often discussed your 'InSystems' technology as a moveable singularity as opposed to a technology singularity. You are a less efficient expression in the goal for a predictable and successful human future. You won't understand this, I suppose... you are still essentially human." the clock muttered.

"Thanks, Pele. That's very reassuring. Talk about back-handed compliments." Esteban scowled.

"No, think about it... You're all humans investing in technology in a piece-meal fashion. Grafting cyber ware, interfacing with AI at your own pace... haphazard and short-sighted, selfish."

The Doctor strapped herself into a seat facing Esteban, "But... the GEN clades can be channeled. You have some of the finest genes concentrated into intellectual paths and harnessed to deliver to a specific goal... whatever that goal may be. Their technology advancements have been astounding over the last fifty years compared to the clunky InSystems modifications."

"Thank you so much Doctor." Esteban's lip twisted.

"Oh Esteban, stop being so dense…" she frowned.

"Yes, let her finish. I had not considered this avenue." Pele peered at them from the cockpit while the Dome folded open, sifting dust.

"… So, the OutSystems announce their assemblies of the 4th to the 9th Fleet immediately after these guys have been killed… but nobody has noticed these guys aren't around anymore. The Roles that these individuals represent have been compromised to an unknown extent…"

"The EarthGov President is running around trying to get them to agree to stay, so he's really busy with that, but no longer seems to have any influence with them… I think you're onto something there, Doctor." Pele's face registered some surprise.

Esteban thought furiously "All the while, the big Political movers and shakers are either on their way out of the Solar System on a jaunt to Arcturus, or are halfway to terraforming Luna…"

"… or are building a space elevator to further reduce the OutSystems monopoly on Earth manufacturing." Pele banked the shuttle, hovering while the Dome closed, pointing it's nose towards the Tharsis Massif.

"Any of those are enough reason in them, how about all of them, or two out of three?" The Doctor sighed.

"Until we know for sure, we can work with those theories. Adjust them as we go." Pele concentrated on the shuttle.

Esteban thought he'd stick with what he knew for now, "Can I see the met-sat updates?"

"I'll browse and cache them from the shuttle rather than have you make a direct connection session." Pele nodded.

"Sure, just stream them to my Veep-queue as soon as they're down. I'll run analysis while we're on approach and see what I can do for them." Esteban settled back in his seat.

"You're from here, aren't you?" she asked him.

"*Si*, Doctor. I suppose it used to be my home." Esteban nodded.

"You don't look like you're happy to go back." she remarked, watching him.

"It's funny…" Esteban sighed, "When I was a boy the city was pounded nine months of the year with hurricanes and high tides, so EarthGov builds us a self-contained, sealed environment to move into and out of the buildings of the city. Once we're sealed and safe from the elements, we're effectively locked in, there's nowhere to go… maybe for thousands of years. Luckily, other cities feel this way. We strap rockets to our city, join the 3rd Fleet off-planet and fly to Mars for a better life. We all think that one day in my own lifetime, we can walk outside in the sunlight again."

"I think that's why most of the first Fleets left." The Doctor grimaced, "We got tired of being punished by a Planet that wants revenge on us for doing what we did to it, that is trying to kill you, personally. So instead we move to a place where the planet might just kill you, but it's not personal this time, and we can fix it instead of breaking it."

Esteban grinned, "I was born when the city was being pounded by the weather, now I'm returning to that city as it's being pounded by the weather."

"You really are the Cartagena weatherman." Pele shrugged.

"You say it like it's fated." Esteban whispered, "Like it's all I'll ever be… that's left of me… will ever be."

The silence stretched in the shuttle as Pele skimmed the hills to the approach.

Cartagena rose out of the foothills like a rugby ball, matt-grey against the wall of rust-yellow haze that formed a wall over the horizon, the storm-front.

There wasn't enough moisture in the thin Martian air to form a mud or to cling to the dust particles, as the swirling storm reached ever further towards the Planita; but there was enough to feed the ever-expanding whorl with warmer damp air to charge these grains with electricity. Spectacular lightning snaked through the belly of the front as it bore down on the first wall of rock to check its relentless, expanding fury.

Briny water sucked from the swampy lowlands and thrown into the upper atmosphere froze quickly, falling back with other particles of frozen carbon-dioxide, displacing the warmer band of air and pushing it further and further away from the eye of the storm.

In the thin air, the granules could reach astonishing speeds; abrasion and lightning were the biggest threats to human settlements and structures.

Fortunately, the shapes and tensile strength of materials manufactured on Earth against its violent weather was equal defense against Mars. The football shape of the 200-story structure presented the same degree of exposure to any prevailing winds, smaller surfaces at the base taking the brunt of the fastest moving grit, while the swollen mid section easily deflected the strongest winds as it slowly rotated on it's central axis.

Storm lightning and other electrostatic discharge from the shimmering horizon-wide maelstrom fed the cities hungry charge-capacitors and batteries, permitting electro-magnetic plating and shielding for the duration.

Esteban could imagine all the indie med-mechs that Cartagena was notorious for, rubbing their hands in glee and cranking up their inverters to full capacity. Their results may have been of excellent quality, but their methods were more than a bit questionable. Esteban thought he should know something about that, personally. Pele slipped the shuttle into a private low berth as the city turned to leeward and sealed the docking bay as soon as they were clear. "Stick to Panglish while we are here Pele, they don't like any of the Newlang patois, okay? Even if you're tempted, just don't."

"Sure, I'll keep that in mind." The clock nodded. "Let us sneak into our hotel rooms and I'll begin my update with my Starmind core. That should take a few hours, if I'm going to do it secretly."

"I'm hungry for some Cartagena fresh food." Esteban stretched out of his seat. The Doctor set the med-mech to 'follow-me' and retrieved a small personal luggage from the locker next to Esteban's. He quickly tugged on some clothing, having disposed of his ruined Pringles in the Argyre and not really needing to wear anything else while he was there.

He had three elaborately-patterned one-piece all-weather suits and two synth-lambskin sets of knee-length boots in small backpack he had put on, to free his hands. "For some or other reason I could eat something different than what I've had the last few days."

The taxi-pod arrived at the hangar and deposited them at the level of their hotel quickly enough.

Their check-in was going smoothly until the lights dimmed to low. The insanely attractive check-in clerk smiled apologetically and announced the city was on lock-down.

Pele shrugged and produced Platinum Credit, and suggested that it would be fine if their suites' bookings were extended to cover the storm. "Just put anything on the rooms, we'll settle when this is all over. You should charge the set rate up front."

Esteban stifled a grin, Cartagena's were notoriously accommodating when it came to Platinum Credit.

"Certainly, Pilot…" The clerk ran the validation with a practiced flick of his wrist, "… and Mister Perez, if you need any additional sleeping linen or pillows, please just call the desk and ask for Martin."

"Thank you so much, Martin." Esteban smiled back with his 'reassuring smile', "Not tonight, but you can never tell with the weather. Tomorrow is a distinct possibility."

"You're most welcome, sir. I'll be here." Martin dragged his eyes over Esteban's body slowly.

"We'll find our own way up, it's been a long uncomfortable day for flying." Esteban stepped towards the escalator.

"As you say, sir. I trust you will enjoy your stay." Martin grinned and set about to help the next in line.

"I think I may, at that." Esteban grinned again and loped to catch up to Pele and the Doctor.

Esteban noticed something about Cartagena, now that he had spent nearly fifteen years in high society, the primary colors were a bit too garish, the materials were slightly frayed; a light globe hadn't been replaced… Cartagena was quaint, provincial.

Cartagena wasn't where the real money was. An esteemed and useful partner in the Fleet, sure. An equal rubbing shoulders with the 1st and 2nd Fleet settlers…? Certainly not.

Esteban ducked under a bulkhead as they padded through the plush synthwool-carpeted corporate suites to their adjoining rooms. His skull was perilously close to the ceiling once they had left the public hall landing and the foyer, and Esteban had to stoop while moving around in a space for the first time since he had left the city all those years ago.

Pele had found a clock-dock in the middle room and set himself up on charge and data, while the Doctor took the end room.

Esteban stretched out on the large bed, his calves extended off the mattress. Sighing, he lay diagonally and managed to fit. Staring at the ceiling, Esteban tried to access the Channels, but there was only local content, and a cached update on the Earth space elevator's Plumb-port nearing it's final position from sometime in the last two months.

Local news had the latest lines of upgraded cyber-model optics, both in materials and color ranges; upgraded A and B skeletal-weave frames, and a version update of a new range of neural-bus compositors.

Cartagena was adapting their earth-tech to lower gravity conditions, different light levels and a new range of materials, including graphene and rigid gels, geocrete and alloys.

Esteban sighed, they were prosperous in a way that could not be on Earth. The Mega-corporation that represented Cartagena showed year-on-year growth and the various subsidiary organizations were liquid and more or less equitable.

Their cyber ware and med-mech was in demand, and their reputation was solid for the many numerous small scale production shops. What if the OutSystems dragged out their nanotech foundries and drove places like this out of business?

What if the human Standard med-mech was squeezed out by the OutSystems flesh-tech? They didn't make things for people, they just grew more flesh and printed it from their portal-wombs and tanks into different configurations.

While all together on Earth, Gravity Well economics meant that the market items cost more or less the same to ship out of the Gravity Well. Up in space where there was no Gravity, the tholin and ooze raw materials were more suited to OutSystems cloning technologies than Earth-Standard augmentation technologies.

The markets were open, demand would shift to cost-sensitivity; and the InSystems Arcology would be finished. The last blow to an already fragile culture would be dealt. Esteban breathed out slowly, thinking. Ooze and Ice production, super-conductivity and the basis for their manufacturing followed a chemical restraint on heat. The OutSystems technologies could only come into full swing inside the chemical limit for Nitrogen Ices.

Esteban rubbed his face. Weather was a combination of electricity, chemical elements and heat systems. Throw in Geology to steer, constrain or channel moving atmospheres and fluids... expand it over a wide area, and simplistically... you had weather.

If human economies ran like weather patterns, and if you took the OutSystems strengths into account... then Esteban could eliminate Venus, Earth itself, Luna, Mars and Ceres from anyone with probable cause to shift the OutSystems economy and manufacturing strengths. It couldn't be too dark, or too cold...

Neptune, Pluto and Uranus were not probable, everything was too small-scale and there was nothing particularly valuable to mass-produce out there, except fusion fuel. But if you had abundant fusion capabilities, you didn't need the OutSystems.

Jupiter and Saturn were the only candidates to engineer something on this scale. They had vast resources that they could exploit, limited only by the speed of their ability to process it… it had to be.

Somewhere in those two planetary Systems, someone was plotting to end Esteban's livelihood, his City's livelihood and his very fragile InSystems culture. Somebody was preparing to make a mockery of the very reasons the first Fleets had fled Earth. No… not if he could do anything…

"Esteban?" The Doctor's voice intruded on his thoughts.

"*Si?*" Esteban opened his eyes and propped himself up on his elbows.

"Do you want to go for a meal? You said you were keen." she was wearing a simple tunic, set with 3-D holograms that cascaded over the smart fabric in the latest fashionable montage, currently popular in Cadiz.

"I am. Sorry, I was just thinking how we're on the very edge of Martian life out here. How the storms rage and how very fragile we all are."

"How so." she blinked.

"I'll just change, do you mind?" Esteban reached for his backpack, "It doesn't go well to be seen stepping out in the same thing you were wearing during the day."

"I've seen it all before, go ahead." she smiled at him.

Esteban tugged off his coverall. "When the 3rd landed, we headed for the highlands, we needed metal and ores… But MF3-Mumbai headed up north, and settled in the flat plains. They were keen for farmlands. It was all they could think about. But their Arcology was stressed, they had packed it with thousands beyond its safe capacity for the trip to Mars." Esteban smoothed his penis flat in the suit and pressed the seal button at the base of his spine. The garment slowly folded closed as he flexed and shifted for comfort. The smart fabric glimmered and scrolled images matching hers.

"They only saw the land, they didn't think that as the soil heated up, the plains would turn to swamp. Technically, the permafrost would warm to quicksand and then liquify. MF3-Mumbai started to bend on it's spindle and then just broke apart in the first big northern storm. They had not reckoned that they had landed on top of a frozen ocean that would one day be tens and hundreds of meters under water. They wanted to solve a problem now, and hang the consequence."

"All Martians know this. The 'Mumbai tragedy' was the worst loss of human life on Mars, ever."

"It's a train of thought, let me finish." Esteban grumbled.

"Go ahead." she smiled again.

"The survivors moved to the foothills below us on the Tempe Terra, away from the plain and set up homesteads… Esteban tugged on his boots, "they had nothing left… but these guys had made it here. We contracted them for mine labor, helped set up ruggedized homesteads and gave preferential rates on GM cereals. Now most of the food in MF3-Cartagena is some of the finest and freshest on Mars. Our school programs for them provided some of the finest technicians we have. What I've learned is that these guys are committed. There is no other option for them.

"Their archaic hunger for land was an just an expression of status that was achievable from a limited perspective… an Earth perspective. On Mars it meant nothing, nobody had the skills for Mars agriculture."

"I hope this train moves on quickly, Esteban. You must be starving."

"The other Arcology treat them like… meat, spare parts. I think that if Mars is going to succeed, we should learn some lessons from what people are doing on the edge of the world to make it work."

"That's… a very nice thought Esteban." She moved to the door and opened it.

"They're adapted to our type of InSystems, they've contributed back to MF3-Cartagena in a way that has forced adjustments in both our mindsets. Where they lived on Earth for thousands of years, the son of a farmer would only ever be a farmer; here on Mars a farmers' son could be a lawyer, an engineer or anything they have aptitude for... because MF3-Cartagena needs skilled labor." Esteban ducked under the doorframe and sauntered towards the restaurant with the doctor.

"There's a 'but' here, Esteban. You wouldn't be chewing this bone for this long if there wasn't one."

"InSystems must completely assimilate them before we become identified with their misfortune, and treated in the same way that they are. Their initial way lies with subsistence and even further isolation. Individuals that are isolated and ignored have no chance by themselves. Being on contract and being indentured, or being viewed as a 'thing' are almost the same thing these days.

"If a culture is to survive, it needs to take care of its collective individuals. If an individual is to survive, they have to maintain and invest in 'their' culture... and that's what I'm not getting a sense of, from the Mega-Corporations and Mega-Collectives that the InSystems Arcology are represented by."

The Doctor stepped off the escalator on the mezzanine landing. Esteban was relieved he could stop stooping. "All I'm getting from them is more and more outrageous displays of arrogance. It's like they're eating their own shit, but they're forcing us to dig around in it for whatever we need before they eat it."

"That's a delightful thought before your dinner." she smiled.

"I'm using 'shit' as a metaphor for the economic and social relationship, Doctor. Consumers don't choose the Corporation production strategy. If all they have access to is shit, then they'll eat it, wash in it, decorate their homes with it and be happy that they have so much of it. Anyway, here we are."

"Esteban… what is that smell…? Its wonderful."

"Ah, that's the carvery. There's lamb, turkey and ostrich, leafy greens and cheeses… Our pride of place is potatoes. Mars and potatoes were made for each other. Have you never eaten fresh produce before?"

"No, MF1-Cadiz only has processed food."

"I think we'll start you with small samples first. Follow me…"

"Oh, I've eaten too much."

"You haven't touched a thing!" Esteban gestured at her plate, "Not really more than a teaspoon of anything, it's the variety that makes your gut think so. Different rates of digestion give you the illusion of being full."

"How long are we likely to be on lockdown?"

"It depends… We're thickening the atmosphere, essentially dragging moisture out of the soil while we're heating the planet… It used to be weeks of global dust, now it's just short of that. I mean, look at MF1-Cadiz and MF1-Marseilles in the Hellas. In a hundred years the air pressure at the bottom of the Planita is half of that of earth-standard, you've got running water into a pooling lake.

"At the top of the Hellas crater, and most elsewhere, the air pressure is five percent at worst, or ten percent on average. In another hundred, you'll live on the shores of a sea that's the size of... the Antipodean Ocean on earth, you know the one that used to be the Arctic Ocean, when north was still north. So weather in the Hellas is more like weather."

"What do you think? You're the weatherman." she pressed him for an answer.

"Maybe another two days? It's been sweeping south for about a week already, so there's not much more to sustain it once it buttresses against Tharsis. It should drop all the ices really soon, which would then slowly melt and universally cool the atmospheric layers to an equilibrium different from the hotter, wetter air and the underlying thicker, cooler moving wedge.

"All the GM lily-pads have been also been disrupted. They'll land and seed where they fall, but while they're been blown about in the storm, their dark color will trap more heat from the sun while they're up there, and they'll rot where they land."

"Decomposition usually involves some heat." she pushed her plate away from her.

"Yes it does, in another decade the whole Boreal Planita will be swampy. When the permafrost goes it'll release methane gasses in huge quantities, more or less at once. That doesn't seem likely during this storm, so factor the lilies into the equation, two... maybe three days."

"That's something to look forward to." Doctor snorted. "Eruptions of rotting vegetation gases."

"Most of the homestead ranchers and farmers should be safer by then, permanently relocated along the higher plains of the Tempe Terra when that happens... I hope. MF3-Cartagena must transplant the MF3-Mumbai claimants to fulfill their allotments as quickly as possible. As soon as that is done, we will be twice the size of any single landed Fleet Arcology.

"If we can show the utilization and development of the Marscape we gain more say in the Martian tribune, according to the Senatorial Charter. MF3-Mumbai was doomed from the start, they chose all the wide open land that was easiest to allot to their tenants… not realizing that all of the Northern plains would eventually become sea-bottom as Mars warmed. They hoped it would take centuries, not the decades the land is submerging at the current rate.

"Are you saying MF1-Cadiz's hydroponics don't count in that allotment equation?"

"Not really, it's mostly automated and it consumes limited resources from the city. You're on the canyons above the Hellas lake. You would need human settlers along the shore to get your extensions. EarthGov's Charter rewards settled humans consuming resources with Tribune seats… wait a minute…"

"What?" she looked up as he dialed a privacy-secure shield around their booth.

"How many Tribune seats would the EarthGov cede to that Terraformer Australian during the transfer…

the one that Pele mentioned?" he said softly as the background noise vanished under the shield.

"I don't really know, our 'net is on lockdown so I can't check."

"I know of at least ten facilities... so... he gets to start in Mars with maybe a dozen seats." Esteban leaned forward.

"That's more than the number of cities on Mars. You think this is what it's all about?" she matched his hushed tone of voice.

"Doctor... this is news, this is a breaking story. We might be getting a Martian Senator!" Esteban whispered excitedly.

"Esteban... just think on what you're saying... If that... Argyre thing... gets out, he'll be indicted in some or other criminal case and his assets would all be foreclosed. This is too big for us. We can't let this slip out." The Doctor waved her hands in a 'down boy' motion.

"You're right. As soon as Pele is finished uploading, we'll have to speak to him. See what he plans to do." Esteban sat back in his seat and pondered.

"How many Senators are there currently?" she sipped her water, looking at the translucent shapes beyond their shield.

"Earth, Venus, Jupiter and Saturn at present. There's talk about a seat for Luna and Ceres coming up, especially in the next few years when Luna has para-terraformed. As soon as that Dome goes up, it's eligible for one. They could pressurize that whole place in twenty years flat out. Ceres is almost entirely dependent on Luna for supplies and shipping, but if Mars were to come on-board..."

"... It would break the deadlock between the Gas Giants and Earth." The Doctor nodded, "Or re-align Ceres to Mars... or to Jupiter."

"Exactly!" Esteban whispered, "Whatever happens, things get to move and shake."

"... Or it would balance out a single Luna-Ceres candidate seat, either way." she sighed deeply. "So if the OutSystems flee Earth, then it's the Jovian's... and if they stay, then it's the Terrans? That seems overly simplistic. Real life isn't usually like that."

"I suppose when you say it like that, it sounds stupid." Esteban groaned.

"That might be so." The Doctor stood and Esteban dialed down the shield, "That doesn't mean you're stupid, unless you want to shout that out to everybody you meet. That would be stupid... and unwise."

Esteban stood and motioned to the waitron "Cheque, please!"

A couple staggered towards where Esteban stood, "I know you, you're that weatherman from 'MCN Naked Weather'. We're subscribers."

"Hullo there. Yes, I'm Esteban Perez." he looked them over, both were young and obviously high.

"I'm Heinz and this is Anne." Heinz grinned at Esteban, "We've just got married, we're on Honeymoon in Cartagena."

"Well, congratulations!" Esteban smiled his 'special smile' at them, "I hope you are happy for a long time together."

"So, ask him already!" Anne giggled at Heinz, "Go on, you said you would. For me."

"Okay [hic] O[hic] kay." Heinz grinned at Anne, "So go on take it out, let me see it."

"I'm sorry?" Esteban could feel his smile freeze on his face, "What?"

"Your co[hic]ck." Heinz pointed at Esteban's crotch, "Take it out. I have an application on my subscriber account that's been granted by MCN. Look here..." Heinz shared a token from his internal mail queue."

"Oh, I see." Esteban checked the authenticity, and took a deep breath, "Sure thing, Heinz. Might I say on behalf of MCN that we value every subscriber from MF1-Bremen." Esteban reached back and pressed the seal of his suit, which peeled off of him and gathered at his ankles.

"*Mein Gott in Himmel...*" Heinz blinked and reached for it, "Here we go, my darling. I'm going to make it rain for you, all over you. Just li[hic]ke you asked for."

"Oh [hic] you're the best, Heinz." Anne clapped her hands and bared her breasts as Heinz closed both hands around Esteban's girth and started to pump.

Esteban was grateful that his skin couldn't blush, he half-closed his eyes as Heinz tugged on his foreskin, rubbing and retracting it, squeezing his girth and rolling it with his sweaty hands.

Out of the corner of his vision, he could see the Doctor watching him clinically; the waiters expressions and those of the other diners... some with horror, others with disgust and a few with appreciation.

Esteban checked the MCN token Terms and Conditions, then dialed up his UroQt orgasm sensitivity to maximum, why prolong this any longer than was necessary?

Esteban groaned as his ejaculate erupted. The first and second jets covered Anne's breasts, her face, her new husbands face, hands and his suit; the third arced over them and spattered over a table cloth of the elderly couple dining behind where they stood, the fourth to the sixth of his spasms splashed to the floor with a series of thudding sounds.

Esteban panted as he announced to them, "MCN appreciates your continued subscriber loyalty" as his knees trembled and he struggled to stay standing. He might not have bothered as the newlyweds kissed each other fiercely, smearing each other with his fluids... but a contract was a contract and he had fulfilled his part.

The waitrons' clean-up crew swarmed down the aisle as Esteban pulled his suit up and sealed it and moved past the tables to the pay-station. Two security clocks were escorting the nearly-oblivious newlyweds out of the restaurant in a tangle of limbs and lips, and the senior waitron was drawing a privacy shield about the gesticulating elderly couple. Esteban couldn't meet anyone's eyes; and under his synthetic skin, he could feel his cheeks and ears burning like fire. A small hand folded into his and he looked down as the Doctor tugged him towards the pay-station.

"Put the cheque to our rooms, please. You know who we are." she smiled as the man nodded, then she lead Esteban outside into the bustle of the deck.

"A contract is a contract," Esteban whispered as they strolled towards the Promenade square. "is just a contract."

"Is a contract." The Doctor found a stone bench around a faux-stone carved fountain, "Esteban I am a med-mech, I know all about contracts. There is nothing sacred about the human body anymore, we're tweaking it, adding to it, replacing it... whether it's metal, or graphene or in synthetic flesh.

"We're adding useful skills and we are selling them to the highest bidder. We are having the Mega-Corporations martialing our expertise and trading products with other corporate collectives... there's no mystery left."

"We are the commodities and we need to do what we can to make ourselves useful." Esteban nodded, still holding her hand.

"Esteban, I can tell you honestly that I don't know where your head is." she gently retrieved her hand.

"That's because you're my med-tech, not my shrink." Esteban clasped his hands between his knees and stared at the faux-cobblestones.

"Yes, my contract is to guard your body from harm," the corner of her mouth quirked, "not anything else. A contract is..."

"A contract, is a contract..." Esteban sighed and leaned back, "Do you even like me, Doctor?"

"You're not really my type, Esteban." she shrugged.

"What? More a clock than a human..." Esteban groaned.

"Not that... more male than female."

"Oh... ?" Esteban blinked in confusion, "Ooooh... so that's why there's no kids!"

"Apparently I'm more competitive in our Group's leadership roles than I should be. It's not that I want to be treated 'special', Esteban. To your point earlier, I want to be treated like me. Nothing more."

"I'm..." Esteban began.

"...insensitive? Self-absorbed? Volatile, impulsive... ?" The Doctor grinned.

"I was going to say 'sorry'," Esteban grinned back, "but you covered it nicely, I think."

"I think so too, not the traits of a clock or a doll or any *thing*." The Doctor looked away at the Promenade with it's throng of gently strolling young people. She registered some surprise at the number of women gathered, about one in three. Cadiz Promenades was seldom more than one in seven.

"So Pele wanted me to let people know I'm here, so I should at least go out tonight. Are you keen to come with?" Esteban followed her gaze.

"Where-ever you go, I go." The Doctor fidgeted her hands in her lap, "That's the contract."

"There's something I need to do, and there's something I'd like to do." Esteban stood and started to walk, "So I'm going to do it."

"You are an impossible cunt sometimes, you know that?" she trotted to catch up with him.

"Part of my charm, Doctor." Esteban shrugged, "A charm that is, apparently, wasted on you."

When Esteban realized he couldn't shake the Doctor, he slowed his annoyed pace and they walked together to the taxi pods and beyond that route, down the crowded decks the transport deposited them. Gang-tags in fluorescent dye tagged the entrances to side-shoot alleys as he meandered down the lanes, when he noticed the Doctor becoming more agitated with each step. "It's okay," he whispered to her, "I have some cred here, it's where I'm from." She nodded at him, but didn't say anything, so Esteban continued his journey until it lead to a door in a hive-street in an alley that was more luminescent tags than any other color.

Esteban rapped at the door in a special way and whispered to the speaker next to it, *"Mama, es Esteban..."*

Esteban waited longer than was necessary, the door finally slid open and they stepped inside. Esteban stooped to get inside and stayed stooped as he lead her up a low ceiling-staircase, bent almost double.

A woman waited for them upstairs, dressed all in black with daubs of white lace at her wrists and throat.

Her hair was tied back in a severe bun and the lines of her face and at her throat appeared to be etched into her skin.

"Oh, boy is she in a mood..." Esteban silently beseeched invisible powers as he kissed his mother's offered cheek, gestured to The Doctor and made the introductions, "Mother, this is Doctor da Silva; Doctor, this in Senora Evita Perez."

"Senora, pleased to meet you." The Doctor ducked in a short courtesy.

"I am pleased to meet you, Doctor." Evita pulled up a chair for her, "What are you doing with this one here?"

"We're working together for a time." She pulled up a chair and perched next to the Senora.

"Oh." Evita's face fell, as she poured a mint tea for The Doctor and pushed a plate of ginger shortbread biscuits over the table." "I'm sure he will disappoint you as well."

Esteban cleared his throat, pulling a low bench towards the table. His knees scraped the underside of the tabletop.

Esteban sipped at the tea, and nibbled at a biscuit. "Have you heard from father? Kept up with any news since I moved to Cadiz?"

"Ramon still stops in once a week to visit. He's the only one of your friends that has kept in touch since…," she waved a hand in his direction, "my boy abandoned his family and his friends."

"Mama, we've been through this before. Every time I stop over in fact. If Papa and I hadn't taken contracts, we would never have been able to come to Mars. Cartagena would never have joined the fleet, we needed the skills to keep us alive on the trip over."

"And you threw away everything we have been for hundreds of years, our culture, our way of life…"

"… Is gone, mama. All of the life we had on Earth before The Ebb, all of the InSystems we crafted to keep us through the Plagues to stay on Earth… is gone.

"So is my family. It was my husbands duty to provide for us. It was *your* duty to make sure he has another family to come back to. One of your own."

"Mama… I like being the me I am now. Not all of it, but…" Esteban sighed, "Okay mama, I'm going to go now. I will stop by again, maybe Easter. Maybe next time we could just talk. Maybe next time we could just talk, maybe about something different… just talk to me"

"Do what you want, Esteban." Evita picked up lace bobbins, "You always do."

Esteban snorted in exasperation, stood in the cramped space and stomped towards the door. "See you at Easter, mama. Take care."

Evita shrugged and said "It was nice to meet you Doctor da Silva."

"And you too, Senora Perez." The Doctor nodded as Esteban squeezed down the staircase, "Thank you for the tea." and started after him.

"He will break your heart, doctor." Evita said softly from her lace bobbins, "It's what he does best."

"Not mine, Senora." She smiled at the woman. "All I care about is that he's safe while he's with me."

Esteban waited for the doctor outside the quarters, staring at the narrow parts of the level. The cramped houses nestled along the narrow faux-cobbled lanes, three storied and crowded in the lower levels, the poor levels. "She hasn't spent a cred of anything I've sent her since I left for MF1-Cadiz. Ramon says she's waiting for my father to finish his contract before she'll leave this house. I send him creds as well to keep an eye on her."

"Wow, what was that about?" she looked up at Esteban, the light shimmering from his suit gave his skinweave a waxy sheen.

"We made choices." Esteban's lips pursed, "We weren't rich enough for Corporate passage, Papa was an Engineer Professor at the University, Mama was in fine arts. Cartagena had dumped almost all of their Mark-2 stock to lighten the lift. The few Mark-3's that were ready had the new anti-psychosis sculpt-masking designed for release. They assigned me the Pondsmith Mark 3 in line with the allocation I requested for the Fleet and Arcology hydrology maintenance until Mars-fall. Papa…" Esteban trailed off.

"Where is your Father?" The Doctor fell in step as Esteban ambled down the lane.

"In the Belt." Esteban shrugged, "He took a full body conversion Mitsubishi-96, Mark 2, one of the last of the Range. It's all still chrome… he worked on the hulls in the flight over and other assemblies and arrays. Once we landed, we still had huge overdrafts to manage. We had to put out our contracts to all-comers."

"MCN took up yours, what about your father?"

"A Thirty year EarthGov contract based in the Asteroid Belt." Esteban sighed, "He maintains the Belt Orbital's and the Ceres Dome. He has thirteen more years on his contract before he gets rehabilitated from his 'Borg transplant. His whole body and some parts of me are in deep storage in the family freeze locker." Esteban trudged down a narrow set of steps while the strips of LED's lighting the passage pulsed erratically, the storm beyond running juice into the inverters. An old, grubby woman sat beside a low table decked with fresh produce, sweets, booster chips and vape-sticks.

A fat brown rat scuttled behind her, unnoticed in the cobbled gutter. Esteban blinked, he'd almost forgotten that rats and pigeons were in MF3-Cartagena everywhere that humans were. The last two decades he'd been living in MF1-Cadiz and they had sparrows and cats. His twice annual visits to MF3-Cartagena weren't frequent enough to make rats part of his cityscape once again.

Esteban selected a candy lollipop and tapped over a few extra creds from his smart-sleeve.

"*Muy gracias, Esteban.*" She grinned at the cred tap. "As generous as always."

"*Es nada, senora.*" Esteban grinned around the candy-stick. "You make the best candy."

"You see Doctor, the rates for EVA welding and vacuum engineering are so much better than any aquatics. If MCN didn't pick me up and strap this horsecock on me, I'd still be looking for work. On Earth, Cartagena is now a two meters-deep bay, between the Castle on one shore and the ruined University on the other. There isn't anyone left there to pay for work, and neither Venus nor Mars is buying for oceanography for decades yet. My best bet is for Mars first, though."

"What's this place?" The Doctor looked around the narrow alley and the steps leading down to a sub-level. A garish sign flickered in the alley '*Le Petit Club Nocturno*' and smaller ones with '*danza*' and '*cocteles*' surrounding the main logo.

"It's my friend Ramon's club. I always stop by when I'm here, when I need to let my hair down."

"It looks seedy." She sniffed, unimpressed.

"Inside is better." Esteban shrugged, "Ramon is doing much better than it looks from out here, with what I've been paying him to look after my mother all these years. I have done for seventeen years."

Esteban ducked into a covered archway as he squeezed down the cobble steps. It opened up into a wider portico, where a pair of guards waited before a large door. Esteban spread his arms as best he could while the man patted him down, "Ramon in yet?"

"*Si.*" Light reflected off his optic mount and his chromed cheek plate as Esteban's suit twinkled in the shadow.

"You new here?" Esteban wiggled his hips as the bouncer plumped his groin and clicked his optics, puzzled "It's all me, I promise."

"*Si*, first week. Is this all just *pinga?*" The man cupped the heavy bulge, as Esteban nodded and then just shrugged to wave him past.

The female bouncer looked at The Doctor and folded her arms, "What about you?"

"I'm with him." She shrugged.

"You looking for trouble tonight, lady?"

"No trouble. Where he goes, I go. You get how contracts go." The Doctor stared back at the large woman, unwavering.

The beefy woman hesitated for a few seconds. "I sure do. Okay, but don't make me regret this. Ramon and him go back a long way. He used to be the Boss's *chica*. They're still tight."

"Does he draw any heat here?" The Doctor squeezed past to follow Esteban inside.

"Nope, he's a pussycat. He Zonedances for a set on the private stage, catches up with the Boss, leaves early. Tonight is the annual Zonedance final."

"No worries then, I promise." She smiled back at the muscle.

Esteban waited for the Doctor to join him before he sauntered through the corridors with her at his side. It was still early, there weren't many people crowding the corridors leading to the dance-floors. Esteban preferred it like this and made for the corridor that lead to the smaller venue.

The first stage was ringed by a series of bars and fake-palms, gigantic pitchers of some liquid were being handed over to patrons, crusted with what looked like sugar, resplendent with fruit of some kind and a small umbrella perched in the container.

A Rockjock was setting up his deck while the tables were slowly filling, and muted strains of the latest hob chart hit the background tracks.

Buff waiters wearing little else but a loin cloth and a cape were bussing the small round tables, their smart-fabric shimmering with images and scrolling landscape scenes from the various outposts over the solar system.

"This is the cocktail bar. If a Table can guess the place, they get a free Mojito of the 150cl size." He grinned at the Doctor as he threaded past a waiter shimmering an icy landscape over his cloak. "Enceladus!" he grinned at the baby-faced man.

"Nope." The waiter smiled back, "Nice try, Esteban but you don't get to play anymore. Ramon actually loses money with you."

Esteban laughed, a twinge of nostalgia tugged at his gut. "I'm off my game. Is he in?"

"Yes, he's expecting you. The usual booth."

"What is the game?" The Doctor looked over the squad of waiters. Some of them were still scrolling images, others of them had 'Phobos' and 'Triton' and 'Venus' labeled over their images as they ran their Tables.

"You guess right, you get a free cocktail and that's the name of your waiter for the evening." Esteban tapped on the door to the private section. "It never gets old, every time you come here you can have someone different waiting on you. The cocktails shuttle and reset when everyone is allocated a name. Over there you can see the sign that a Steelworks is next up."

"Like a booze-bingo." she laughed. "Except all the booze is from potato and sugar-beet."

"It's pretty good for what it is, not like that synth-choo that you guys have." Esteban nodded as the door opened for them. "It's exactly that. It's also a way to downsize rationing, get people used to what we had when we crossed to planet-fall on Mars. Getting people used to what we have, when we have it. Ramon is clever that way." Esteban lead her through the doorway. "This is the second dance floor, where other types of customers come. To be more themselves. You need a ticket to get in here. I booked before we left MF1-Cadiz. It was part of Pele's plan to cover our tracks."

The Doctor nodded and followed Esteban down a narrower corridor to where it opened up into a smaller space.

Instead of the dance floor surrounded by bars, this one had booths surrounding it and only a single bar at the far end.

Esteban headed for a booth where a movie-star handsome man waited, his shaven head flickering with mood tattoos. He looked up as they approached, and stood to invite them into the booth.

"*Hola guapo, muy Buena's.*" He reached up to Esteban and tugged his face down for a kiss on the lips.

"*Hola papi chulo, Buena's Noches.*" Esteban smiled and leaned into what became a smoldering kiss.

"You're looking good, the style suits you." Esteban whispered as he finally pulled away.

"You too." Ramon patted Esteban on the haunch, "Mighty fine, like a prize stallion. Are you even bigger than last time? I didn't think you could do that."

"Si, but I can't do that by myself. I had help." Esteban turned and gestured to the doctor, "Ramon, this is Doctor da Silva."

"So, Doctor Senora da Silva, how are you with this one?" Ramon's smile slipped momentarily.

"I'm his contracted Doctor and I take care of his body." She looked over at Esteban. "I'm monitoring a treatment."

"Nothing special?" Ramon smiled at Esteban, "Perhaps the prospect of a rom-"

"Not like that, no." the Doctor shook her head.

"Pity…" Ramon shrugged and clicked his fingers at the barman. A clock walked to where the barman started to assemble a drinks order. "Come sit with me. Tell me what you're doing. You pick a fine storm to visit this time."

Esteban waited for the Doctor to seat and shift before he sank against the bench and stretched out his legs under the table, "One day perhaps, I'll be standing on the beach outside telling you about a storm like this. Not yet, but one day."

"One day soon." Ramon smiled, "It's always been your dream. So what's news?"

"Nothing much, I stopped in by mother." Esteban sighed, "Still the same. How about you?"

"Graciela is pregnant again." Ramon shrugged, looking smug. "Another girl."

"That's three in a row!" Esteban whistled low and pointed at Ramon's lap, "Those are golden balls, right there."

"It's a pity you didn't keep yours." Ramon grinned, "Mamacita would still be talking to you if you had."

"They had no place on this model. It is what it is." Esteban sighed, "But... *three*...? You're going to be married into all sorts of influence before long."

"I guess so, *papito*. I have all sorts of people wanting to talk to me about my marriage plans for them. Some even from the upper levels, we'll just see what the girls have to say about it when the time comes." Ramon looked up at the door as people filed in and sat at booths, "Near full house for tonight's show. You want in?"

"You think I could get a show in? Like usual?" Esteban tucked his feet in as the clock placed a pitcher and glasses on the table.

"Sure thing, I've loaded your Zonedance set." Ramon positioned a mini-deck and plugged a lead into a port at his wrist. "We don't have as much time tonight, want to take what I've got? Thirty minutes to warm up the punters?"

"Sure thing." Esteban grinned gleefully, trotting to the dance floor as a beat increased in volume and the lights changed and dipped "You drive, pump it"

***

The Doctor watched Esteban as Ramon toggled the deck.

He looked up at her "It's a 'classical music' mix that I've build up for him over the years. He has the weirdest taste, so the crowd drops big cred for his show. I stream background content to the waiters smart-cloth capes upstairs, so they know there's a show. I have a surprise guest lined up he doesn't know about."

"Has he always moved like that?" she whispered.

"Oh yes, even before the conversion." Ramon smirked, "It's how we met up on Earth."

"What do you have lined up tonight?" she asked, eyes still locked on the swaying form on the dance floor. The tune throbbed and launched into a scat: *…gengengengengengengengen…*

"For him?" Ramon glanced up and saw her still watching Esteban, "The Marlena Shaw sample, followed by 'Cities in Dust' because we're on Mars. Next we'll 'enjoy the silence' because it's fashionable, then 'It's my life' because he likes to talk-talk. Those ones are great for the crowd upstairs, all those earth-scene shots and animals that nobody has seen for centuries. Last we'll 'Fade to grey' and then finish with his signature tune from Tori and Armand."

"That's not what I meant." She said.

"I know, you'll just have to wait like everyone else." Ramon smirked, "You're recording this, aren't you?"

"Yes I am."

"I thought you were on contract as his Body Guard. Molly at the door sent me through your scans." Ramon toggled on the fade and the waiters and clocks smart-cloth displayed a man with an ermine cloak walking alone with a deck chair through beautiful Earth landscapes.

"Same contractor, different contract." She shrugged "He really can move his hips like a snake."

"That could get messy, juggling contracts." Ramon loaded the smart-fabric buffer queues, "You don't remember us working together before, do you?"

"Details of contracts are confidential. They go into encrypted archives at my personal Compliance Net at the end of the contract. If we ever had a contract, you would know better than to ask."

"As you say, Doctor da Silva." Ramon's fingers danced on his deck, "If you're with him, then he's as safe as he can be." The beat changed and faded into the bridge, *'Oh honey bring it close to my lips…'* "If you don't remember what you did for me, I at least do."

"How long has he been doing this?"

"All along. He takes leave to come here twice a year and Zonedances the crap out of this place. Now I give him the floor and charge tickets. The year's Zonedance finalists get one shot at his crown. Tonight isn't the final he's thinking it is, it is much, much more." A green icon hovered on his deck pending queue.

"How so?"

"It'll be quicker to wait and see for yourself. I suggest you keep your recording on. My Club contract prevents me from recording or broadcasting... but a *private* record of this night, well, that's golden. I let you in tonight because I was veeped a lot of cred to allow this to happen as soon as you showed up, thank you very much." Ramon grinned, on the dance floor Esteban was winding down as the audio throbbed *'size size size size size size…'*

Esteban took a bow and moved back towards the booth. He settled back and reached for a bottle of water, to the Doctor it looked like he was enjoying himself immensely.

Ramon grinned at them, then flicked his deck to projection and his holographic avatar loomed large above the dance floor.

"Buena's Nochas and welcome to Le Petit. Tonight is a spectacular night, we have seen our reigning champion warming up and as you can agree, he is definitely in outstanding

form; muy hermoso. *Who is to challenge him for this years crown, when no-one can come close to his outstanding performance? Who indeed?*

"As to who...? Who better to beat a Student than their Teacher? Who better to knock the crown than someone who handed it over... Tonight, for the first time in twenty-two years a public appearance ... I present for you, our very own La viejita Dona Senora Mercedes and the Flamenco baile."

"No way!" Esteban's eyes were wide with surprise as he whispered.

The Doctor watched as a whip-cord slender figure took to the dance floor in a ruby and turquoise banded dress, with a long frilled tail and with orange ruffles separating the bands.

Her snow-white hair was secured in a hive with ivory combs and trailing strings of jet beads. She took her position in the center stage in the hushed room and after a few moments began with a slow rhythm of castanets, and followed with a more insistent series of taps.

Each arm and head position was precise and measured through long practice, as the rhythm *clikka-casta-clikka-casta-clikka-clikka* rolled, and rolled and then picked up to match the *tocco- tocco-tocco-tocco, plante-plante!* rhythm of her foot work.

"Ole! es baile!" the exclamations from the booth section rattled over the floor.

Her dress tail swept out and snapped like a peacock's tail and swirled back like an enameled bell in a cathedral tower. Multi-coloured glitter-lights woven into the fabric shimmered in time with her movement.

"Ole!" the crowd exploded.

Just when the Doctor thought the woman couldn't possibly add any more craft to the dance, she started a slow pirouette to add to the motion of the tail-snap which lifted the orange ruffles into whirling bands around her body.

The Doctor realized that her jaw had dropped as the castanets rhythm picked up to match the insistent heel thrumming with the crowd exclaiming *ole!* with each dress snap on the arc, *Ole! Ole! Ole!*

Then the Dona Senora raised her arms in a rolling motion as she pirouetted around the floor until her hands and the snapping castanet's were fully extended, *clikka-tocco-clikka-tocco-casta-casta-tocco-tocco-plante!plante!* It was over.

The room was silent for heartbeats and then erupted into cheers and whistles.

Ramon's floating avatar shimmered into view above the dance floors, "We *will count votes for the next thirty minutes, find a waiter or a clock, press your thumb of either of the two candidates displayed on their capes. Starting... now!*"

Esteban trotted to the floor and offered his arm to walk the lady to the booth. She accepted his arm and tread regally beside him to join Ramon and the Doctor.

"You're still magnificent, Dona Senora." Esteban breathed, all grins and smiles. "You haven't changed at all."

"But you have, Esteban." Dona Mercedes ran her hand over his cheek tenderly,

"So *gringo* now... what happened to my dark-skinned blatino genius, who wanted to dance so badly that he persuaded the boss of the thugs that beat him on the way to my studio, to escort him instead."

"I'm still here, Dona Mercedes, under this shell." Esteban's face flickered with a darker emotion, "I did this so that we could all come here. My father, too. Without what we did, there was no joining the Fleet."

"Now you and me and your thug are here, together on Mars. The gravity favors my knees for one more dance like this. Ramon told me that you were coming tonight, and I knew this was my last chance."

"For what Dona Mercedes?"

"If I win tonight, Esteban, then you will dance the Mapalé with me. That will be my last performance ever."

"But… we last danced on earth, before everything… and the Fleet. That was over twenty years ago…"

"Yes, the last Mapalé danced on Earth, and the first to be danced on Mars. Some things Cartagena must keep alive, to honor our traditions."

"Dona Mercedes, it's been twenty-"

"Esteban! The Mapalé is a dance performed by slaves on the river among the reeds, a celebration of surviving in a new land, of the fish that fed them and the sex that strengthened their bonds." Dona Mercedes sipped at a cocktail, "The Mapalé is in your blood, many generations of dancers lead down time and place to you. I have never seen a better Mapalé dancer, before or since. When I take this crown, you will dance with me for Cartagena and on Mars. Your body will remember the dance."

"You mean *if*, Dona Senora Mercedes." Ramon shrugged. "You were over eighty on Earth already."

"No, my sweet little thug with your heart of gold," Dona Mercedes smiled and patted his cheek, "I mean *when*. Besides which, I've always shaved a few years off my age. I'll get changed for the set. Excuse me."

The Doctor watched, her lenses etched with the miserable look on Esteban's face.

"She's not joking. She was never one to dabble with uncertainty." Ramon smiled, "She's pulled ahead on votes and it's unlikely she'll lose this now, Esteban. What do you need?"

"How about that loincloth on Charon over there?" Esteban gestured, "At least I'd get to see him in the buff if I take it."

Ramon gestured and the young man came over, as Esteban kicked off his boots and slipped out of his suit, "I'm sure she knew that watching you dance always made me hard, that I'd have you in the garden before I'd walk you home. I just get to look at you now."

"I miss those days, to be honest." Esteban secured the loincloth, "It doesn't have to cover me, I suppose. It represents the poverty of the enslaved. I could just as well be naked, or in a reed skirt. Ramon, I'm not sure I can do this anymore." Esteban sighed and hung his head, "That the conversion…"

"Esteban!" Ramon whispered insistently, "Listen to me. You're bigger and stronger than you have ever been, you're been sculpted to perfection. You're still you, still meat and blood under all that synthwork. The youth born to the Mapalé. Dona Mercedes has never been wrong about you… or about me, for that matter. Trust yourself, get to the place where we used to go together after the dancing, in the garden. Start from there."

"So Doctor, do you think I should do this?" Esteban looked over to where she was watching him.

"I think you want to keep Zone dancing, that this is important to you." She shrugged, "You need to stick to the rules to stay in the game."

"It's time." Ramon's fingers danced over his deck. "Dona Mercedes has seventy percent of the vote. I'll post the vote and give her the vox. She wanted to say something first. Are you ready?"

"*Si.*" Esteban gulped from the pitcher. "Let's just do this."

Ramon's avatar danced above the floor, *"You've seen the votes, you've seen the score, friends of LePetit… I present to you the 2226 winner of the Zonedance, Dona Senora Mercedes for her perfect Flamenco baile."*

The Doctor turned to watch as the woman walked to the center of the floor; barefoot in a plain two-piece bikini, a tassel of synthetic horse-hair draped over her firm buttocks.

"Patrons, guests, welcome! Tonight, I challenge the runner up to join me for my last performance. Tonight, we dance the Mapalé … on Mars!"

The Doctor watched as the Dona Senora gestured to Ramon for the lights and the music started. She thought it sounded raw, repetitive a cadence of *ta-Dah-ta, Tah-da-ta, ta-da-Tah-da.*

The Dona Senora spun and swayed, her lithe hips whipping the horse-tail behind her in a manner reminiscent of her snapping flamenco dress as she completed a slow spiral, feet and hips gliding as she spun. She stopped in place of the start of her circuit and swayed slowly as Esteban entered the circle of the dance floor lights, his oak-stain synthetic skin clinging tightly to his heavy musculature.

His thighs bulged as he pumped his feet against the floor and he spiraled as she had, but in the opposite direction. As he reached her position, he sank to the floor and stretched out on his belly, pumping his hips and grinding his groin against the floor.

"The movement imitates sex, as well as the last movements of a landed fish in the mud beside the river." Ramon whispered over the Doctors recording as Esteban rolled smoothly onto his back, planted his feet and pumped his hips into the air with arced back. The Dona Senora stepped over him, swaying and undulating her hips as his heavy phallus swung pendulously and bounced off his taught abdomen.

"There are three more movements from here. Lift, Arc and Swing." Ramon continued softly over the *ta-Dah-ta, Tah-da-ta, ta-da-Tah-da*, "You need strength, balance and a certain familiarity to complete the dance. You'll see."

Esteban rose from his position in a single smooth uncoiling, one moment his back was arched, the next he had rolled onto his feet to a standing position, scooping the Dona Senora with him, her legs outstretched and holding her stance with clasped knees aside his neck.

He spun slowly in place; his arms outstretched and spinning the extended woman from her single contact point on neck and shoulder.

The Doctor nearly blinked at the next passé, but long habit kept the recording clear. Esteban placed a hand in the small of her back and lifted her off his neck and up above his head while maintaining his slow pirouette.

She marveled as he held the Dona Senora aloft, his spine taught, his strength concentrated in a pure line, holding her above him for another series of *ta-Dah-ta, Tah-da-ta, ta-da-Tah-da*.

"Wait for it..." Ramon said quietly.

She gasped as Esteban's buttocks clenched as he pushed the Dona Senora into the air, only to catch her at wrist and ankle and swing her around at his arms length. On the seventh swing, the Dona Senora brought her free knee up and Esteban righted her, released her ankle in a smooth movement and slipped that hand into the small of her back.

He tucked her against his body as he sank to one knee, folding her protectively against the skin of his torso as he extended his right leg behind him.

She draped her bent knee over his thigh and pressed her cheek against his chest on the last *ta-da-Tah-da*. Esteban sank his face onto the top of her head while extending his right arm and stopped moving in that position.

Ramon flipped the lights off as they held in that position.

The Doctor stopped her recording, and blinked moisture against her lenses. "Magnificent." She whispered.

"The Mapalé on Mars." Ramon brought up the lights as the applause rang through the room. "A moment that could only happen here in Cartagena, and will never happen again. This could be a signature piece for humanity on Mars."

"I only take care of his body, Ramon." The Doctor folded her hands in her lap and looked down at the dance floor where the Dona Senora and Esteban were taking their bows.

Esteban kissed the Dona Senora on the cheek as the lights brightened and the applause and whistles rolled out to them. "This is your moment now. Thank you, Dona Senora. I'll be sure to stop by the next time I'm in town." He whispered and left her to the adulation flowing from the booths.

He stepped from the dance floor and made his way back to the booth. Ramon and the Doctor were watching him as he flipped off the leotard and put his suit back on. Charon retrieved it after putting another pitcher into the table and a few liters of water bottles beside it, winked at Esteban and glided back to his tables.

Esteban gulped at the water, not being able to sweat through his synthskin had practical disadvantages that the UroQt only mostly compensated for.

"Doctor, we should go." Esteban smiled fondly at the attention being heaped on the Dona Senora, "The rest of the night belongs to her."

"Take care of yourself, *chica*." Ramon glanced up from his deck, "Let me know when you're back in town."

"I will do, *guapo*." Esteban leaned over and kissed his cheek, "Thank you for setting this up."

They walked through the level in the dimmed light, the rare observation port showed only a dark orange tint as the storm whipped outside and took a pod back to the hotel level. Esteban was silent, a pang of nostalgia rang through him. The Doctor walked beside him without feeling the need to break his silence.

As they walked through the Lobby to check in, Esteban dialed 'expression 26' from his catalogue and collected his key pass from the Front Desk. "Hey, Martin," he smiled at the clerk, "I'm going to need a pillow in about twenty minutes. Do you think you could bring one to my room?"

"*Si*, Senor Esteban." Martin beamed at him. "I'll make the arrangements."

Esteban awoke with a start, his veep channel throbbed with alert queues from Pele. He sat up and threw his legs over the side of the bed amidst the rumpled, stained linen and scattered pillows. His muscles complained pleasantly, and he felt agreeable despite the disturbance.

"What?" he opened his veep channel.

"Esteban! Wake up, we need to get moving." The avatar pulsed urgently.

"What's going on?" Esteban reached for a water bottle and his clothes.

"We've got an alert from the shuttle. Someone has followed us here." Pele buzzed back.

"How do you know this?" Esteban tugged on his boots and sniffed his fingers. He could still smell Martin on his skin.

"I handle all the dispatches, I told me… or rather Starmind_core gave me a heads-up."

"What now?" Esteban felt an icy fear creep up inside him.

"They'll trace the hangar to the hotel booking for this pilot clock. I've got to switch the hotel booking systems to disconnect me from you two in the log records."

"What do we do with your room?" The Doctor joined the veep.

"Set up your diagnostics table there for Esteban. That'll explain the connections and the data use. I'll set up a dummy clock-room and abandon it after a check-in." Pele said after a few seconds of processing.

"I'll get busy on it." she dropped out of the call.

"What do I do?" Esteban finished the water and tossed the bottle into the recycle bin.

"Nothing different, your best cover is that you are doing what you are doing. You know this place well, especially the off-grid places. Where can a clock go to be invisible?"

"*When it's just a doll.*" Esteban mused, "I might know some places… how bad is this?"

"Not too bad. Whatever we've done has triggered something, but it doesn't look like this is a serious alert. I'm going to have to consider a good cover story. I'll leave the hotel now, you go somewhere in about twenty minutes and I'll just follow you there."

"Sure thing." Esteban tugged on his other boot as the adjoining door clicked locked and the dial spun to when they had first arrived. As far as the Hotel-mind was concerned the room had not been used as an 'adjoining room' while they had been here.

"It's done. I've just rolled out the screens on the unused bed and plugged it in." The Doctor waited in the corridor outside as Esteban left his room.

"Have you ever been to the workshops?" Esteban grinned down at the Doctor. "Considering your trade, have you ever wondered where the cyberware is made… also, I feel like some ice-cream."

"I have a feeling you're going to show me." She smiled back. "Lead on."

Esteban sauntered through the levels with the Doctor beside him. It was early enough that there wasn't a throng to push past, and late enough that food vendors had the first of their wares ready. Esteban chunked his way past them, hash browns and strips of rabbit and goat meat, synth-proteins and pseudo-corn burritos, roasted ground nuts, a sugared drink and finally, ice cream. "Don't you eat anything?" Esteban licked his fingers as he scooped the last of the milky liquid from the small cup.

"I eat a lot." The Doctor shrugged as the loitered near the small plaza where the stall was. "Just not so much when I'm on contract. Is that real ice-cream?"

"Yes, it is. I don't know where they get the dairy... or what type of dairy it is." Esteban shrugged, "It's the only place on Mars that I've ever found that does proper ice cream."

"Pele is still shadowing us." The Doctor looked up at Esteban and said quietly, "Where will you take him?"

"How can you tell? I haven't seen him at all." Esteban blinked in surprise.

"I have my means. Trust me, he's here." she smiled.

"I'm going to the foundries, *es mi tochapelotas*." Esteban frowned in annoyance. *Fine then, let her keep her secrets.* "They're below Cartagena itself and set into the bedrock. It's where the furnaces vent all the gasses from the industry to thicken the atmosphere and heat this section of Mars. We have boutique rock-carved warehouses and assemblies, smelters and factories down there. It's a pretty rough place, it's where a lot of the MF3-Mumbai rescues were housed after it fell and they run gangs down there. It's pretty rough if you're not a local but Ramon has a lot of street-cred, so that should extend to us."

"You think the gangs would provide running cover for us?" The Doctor frowned, "That's pretty smart of you."

"I thought so. I'm not just a stud, you know." Esteban grinned. "Come on, let's get a pod. It's still quite a way."

Esteban wasn't exaggerating. The pod sped down the spindle and below the mountings and then some distance horizontally until finally stopping at a chamber where they disembarked.

The tunnel itself was several meters in diameter, and Esteban had more than enough space to move around. "We're going to meet Jose, he's the one who fitted my Pondsmith, way back when. He's a big-time mech, one of Cartagena's finest. He exports off world and keeps a warehouse of dolls to ship to the other Martian Fleet cities. So there are dolls moving in and out all the time. He also uploads soft-personas into them when the demand for clocks pick up, so he is one of the few places where you can get all sorts together. The best place I can think of to hide Pele."

"As I said, smart." she nodded. "Hide in plain sight."

Esteban wove down several branches of the tunnel, dodging wheeled automatons going about there business and work-groups of mechanics and drivers. Almost all of them were slighter and darker than the up-city people the Doctor had seen so far, and almost entirely male.

"Jose is just down here." Esteban waited for an ore-cart to roll past, "He's not the most social of anyone I've ever met, but you can trust him." Esteban blinked away a few thoughts, "Well... if he warms up to you, and there's profit in it... then maybe you can trust him."

"I'll keep that in mind." she grinned, "As it happens I am in the market for a discrete type of mech, both personally and professionally."

"Then you'll be just fine." Esteban fidgeted, "You should be."

The tunnel forked, and at the wedge of the crossroads was a mirrored glass-fronted office that Esteban stopped at. He buzzed at a doorbell, and followed the Doctor inside as it slid open.

A coarse-featured bear of a man waited behind the counter, attachments from his arms zipping over a circuitry component. "Just a minute, please."

"No hurry." Esteban watched patiently as the slender tools retracted back into the forearm pods and the large hands clicked back into the wrist sockets once the housings closed. The optics mask lifted from his face and he blinked in recognition.

"Esteban Perez, the aquanaut." Jose's hoarse voice grunted, "What's up?"

"Hola, ese." Esteban grinned his best smile. "I thought I'd stop by and see how you're doing and bring a friend with to show her."

"You're not here about any warranty, or something?" Jose squinted at the pair. "The Mark 3's are good for fifty years, guaranteed."

"Still so suspicious, you want to look me over for old time's sake. See how it's hanging?" Esteban worked on his most appealing expression.

"Well, you look good. I see you on the MCN every day." Jose shrugged, "Where you get the cock-meat, though? I didn't do that."

"MCN put it on when I signed with them. They said the seam-work was quality, but I always thought one day to come and check with you. Not for gratis... of course." Esteban added hastily, "Just to make sure this work matched your standards."

"Did they enhance or replace?" Jose grunted as he doffed the optic assembly and rubbed his scalp with his flesh-hand.

"Enhance and sculpt." Esteban smiled again, "It's still me, somewhere."

"Who's this?" Jose seemed to relax slightly.

"She's a friend, a Doctor and a med-mech from Cadiz, down by Hellas. We were travelling together for a contract when… you know, the weather." Esteban gestured.

"Esteban thought to bring me along on his trip down memory lane." the Doctor nodded at Jose, "The closest I come to the cyberware at the Clinic is pulling them out of their boxes from a shelf. I need to shop around for them and for myself for more... specialized clients."

"Ah, you never been to a foundry?" Jose nodded, catching the gist.

"No, never. My first time." she shook her head.

"There are rumors in Cadiz that we shave them on the price in Cartagena." Esteban interjected smoothly, "So I say to her don't worry about the supply, I'll show you my connection's warehouse. Your up-and-coming enterprises in Cadiz, sure… they got nothing, they might dip you. Jose is my guy and has been doing this for so long, he's got the stock. Maybe even some retro chrome Earth curios... from before the Fleet."

The Doctor looked at Esteban quizzically, but picked up smoothly, "In Cadiz they say Cartagena has to make every piece on order from scratch, for the amount you charge them."

"Rubbish!" Jose flushed, "They're double-dipping you. I've got the supply, I promise. "Come, I'll show you."

Esteban fixed an expression on his face and veeped Pele on a thin-client channel *"We're here, walk down the corridor, strip down like a doll."*

"What?" Pele's communication sounded indignant.

Esteban sighed mentally, *"Strip your clothes off look like a doll, you'll see your chance to hide. You'll see."*

Jose tapped on a console. "It's not only for Esteban's Mark 3. My contract for Cartagena was for five full-body replacement casings for Pondsmiths. The aquanaut was never a popular model. There's still two waiting for allocation after twenty years. I don't stock too much of what MCN did to his junk either, but I do keep at least one line of my streamlined model of the UroQt. That seems to be the take-away product from all the MCN publicity. I move at least four of the recreational sculpt of those a month in the Fleet markets." Jose tapped on his smart-fabric console, "Just give me a few seconds to set the warehouse lights and you can see for yourself. Most of the work down here is on drone schedules so it's not what you could call 'meat-friendly'."

"Why would that be your lead product? I don't get it." She snorted.

Jose's craggy face split into a grin. "I know, right? I designed the Quart for sub-dermal perspiration and heat transfer in Industrial application. If you have a Mark 3 casing for sealed systems, you have to have a well for fluid transfer. But it turns out every other chaol tops up their kit with the recreational sculpt these days especially if they plan to do off-planet work."

"So I'm an actual Doctor, but I'm not up to date on the gravity connection." The Doctor shrugged, "Are you saying there is an *actual* design condition?"

"Yes. The fluid retention and buildup in the Belt and the Big Dark without the proper gravity lead to hyponatremia, so the last couple years I've moved a lot of the model.

" I didn't call it the 'Doctor Pint', it would dilute the product brand, but now I have every other joyboy, collarboy or chromer wanting to boost their goo with the UroQt-lite in case they contract up there." Jose pointed to the roof.

"Considering the symptoms of hyponatremia, it suddenly makes sense to be able to expel large volumes of fluid. You stay sharper and live longer up there. I never made the connection before." She mused.

"I only kept the Quart model for the full casings, dealing with serious temperature and pressure extremes."

Jose checked his console again, "Ese, remind me if your organ storage is with me."

"No Jose. They're in a family freezer in the Body Bank." Esteban dropped his USSD channel and blinked as he caught up.

"Just as well, the bonelace and marrow stacks leaves genetic markers, unlike the wetware and nanoware modifications, they're inheritable. A Family freezer is safer that way. If OutSystems got control of those glands, they could clone up three meter knockoffs of you any time they wanted; brew an army of license rip-offs."

"I thought of that. Truth is the locker is pretty full already, some skin and a pair of gonads wasn't too much to add and we pay for the volume, not the weight. Dad's in there." Esteban sighed inwardly, Jose didn't appear to have noticed anything out of the ordinary.

"Here we are," The door clicked and Jose rolled it open "My stock room." Racked up in front of them was inert doll after doll in storage frames extending to the back of a seriously big room.

The Doctor whistled quietly under her breath. "It seems at Partridge, Muckagee and da Silva we're getting played by our current suppliers, as you say double-dipped."

"You're with that crowd? Word is your pricing suffers from all your Cadiz half-inchers, and you mostly deal with collarboys."

"Ese! Be nice." Esteban groaned, "The Doctor is doing me a favor… hopefully you as well."

"Maybe, Cadiz tech is good but fickle with fashion changes. If you want good honest reliable tech, then Esteban here is my best work. Quality stuff."

"I'm doing his maintenance now, I agree." She nodded. "Jose, I'll send you a pro-forma and a stock request. Let's see where this leads, you already trump our current suppliers in guarantees, and if we move our procurement upstream we can control our costs as well. Thank you, Esteban for making this happen."

Esteban beamed a quick Instant Message to Pele, *"Now, go now."* While Jose and the Doctor chatted, a quick movement at the doorway and down a corridor of stacking crates was the only sign of the clock that he had seen since leaving the hotel. Esteban felt some relief, so far his plan was working. "Ese, why do you store them as dolls like this?"

"Every piece of my work is complete. If I have to ship a piece, I can keep my inventory updated quickly. Flesh-tech and Cyber-tech need to be complete. There's no reason to do otherwise if you're just spitting out parts."

Jose shrugged as they moved back towards the tunnel, "With the dolls, all I have to do is load a cache and they can deliver themselves. Clocks are harder to work with because once they're embedded with softpersona they have to be powered and maintained. De-commissioning and re-commissioning clocks is a lot of work."

Pele tight-beamed Esteban, *I'm in a frame. I have power and links and I'm going dark. It worked.*

"That sounds more like art, Jose," the Doctor smiled, "and not just tech anymore. There is one last thing I want to run past you, but it's a bit delicate to bring up."

Jose shrugged as he powered down the lights of the warehouse and sealed it, "You can always ask me. If I trust someone, I trust someone. It's what I tell myself that matters."

"It's about a SEAT-09, Mark 3." She looked over at Esteban, "Can you restock remotes for that model?"

"I've never heard of one of those." Esteban shrugged.

"That's a rare and specialized military-hive model." Jose scrunched his face, "Those are very difficult to match, and it depends on the specification of the remote. I can't equip the dolls with gunsmith tech, but I can match clock-control modules and sculpt to specification. That's about as far as I can go with that. Once the remote is docked with the carrier, I know a gunsmith who can complete any job for the rest of it. If your client is worried about discretion, I can vouch for the gunsmith."

"That should be enough to go on." The Doctor nodded, "I'll consult and get back to you."

Esteban checked his sleeve for the time. "You want to look at my junk now?"

Jose nodded, "Sure bring it into my consulting room. Strip down, let's see it."

Esteban sat in the diagnostic chair while the doctor browsed through old news foils and special interest scans, his ankles held high with straps. Even though he was used to examinations, he still felt exposed as Jose ran through his diagnostic tools, especially over the smooth expanse where his scrotum used to be.

"This is quality work from what I can see. They've matched the sub-dermal weave seamlessly to the same specification. I couldn't do it better. Have you noticed any any stress on tumescence?" Jose sat back and disengaged his optics.

"Nope, It gets harder, not bigger. The casing is the determinate. The meat inside conforms to the weave, and it works with the UroQt as a heat transfer vane for high-temperature environments. It was the best I could do within the range of the contract."

"That makes sense. You were always very practical around your conversion." Jose's tools slipped back into their housing with a click and he flexed his fingers absently. "Good solid work and well to specification for the Pondsmith. I'd say you've got another thirty years on your guarantee before you start to risk legacy wear-and-tear, but by then we should be in the Mark-4 or Mark-5 product range so you should have a whole new range of choice."

"Good. I just had to make sure." Esteban dropped the lifts and stepped out of the chair.

"I've got to get back to the aerators for the homesteads. The storm looks like it's almost over so I should get on with it. Will you let yourself out?" Jose nodded to the Doctor and closed the door behind him.

Esteban stepped into his suit as the Doctor hovered by the door "Let's get back to the hotel. The lunch carvery is almost ready."

They threaded through the tunnels before she spoke again: "Esteban, you actually amaze me. Just stop here for a moment. Seriously, stop walking." The Doctor pushed him back against the rock face and looked around.

"How so?" The corridor was suspiciously quiet and Esteban felt a growing sense of unease.

The Doctor looked puzzled... "You are very... human. The Pondsmith upgrade is difficult, one of the most difficult there is. But you've done it. You have to endure the pain of upgrading your size, complications with your bone marrow, complete skin transplant, the sealed systems and all that it entails... and yet I get the sense of a complete person. All the psychological baggage that goes with that, you don't seem to have. How do you do that?"

Esteban lowered his voice to match her tone, "When you dance, you have to get the feel of the movement before you begin. You have to visualize that outcome. Project a perfect execution while you are pushing yourself to match that execution, the ideal you have presented to yourself... you might beat yourself up if there are variations... but you know what your projection is... and you know what your execution is. I did that with the Pondsmith."

She scrolled images on her smart-sleeve, apparently distracted from the conversation, "But other people only see your execution?"

"Yes. I do not think I will ever dance the Mapalé again, exactly like that. It was with Dona Senora that it was perfect. That moment will stand in my life, I will never have chance to return there."

The Doctor looked up at him, Esteban noticed that her eyes had changed color, "Nothing will ever compare? Everything after that is just imitation of perfection?"

Esteban's sense of unease ramped up a notch, "Quite correct. I will never have the same dance partner, I will never have the same sense of urgency and improvisation, I will never be as young or as old as that very moment. It was unique, and to pretend this is not so would be to rob that moment of its importance. What's wrong?"

"All the coms have gone quiet." she looked around again, "The last feed I could harvest was maybe four off-worlders coming on to this level, and the chatter from the local channel is spiking. There is going to be trouble."

"What Pele said?" Esteban nodded.

"More or less." The Doctor nodded, "They've blundered into a situation they weren't expecting. My job will be to get you out of here. I am contracted to guard your body."

"I thought we had covered that by the lake?" Esteban was confused.

"What can I say, I'm versatile." She grinned, "Pele warned me that we could draw a lot of heat, but the primary goal was covert ops. I didn't bring a lot of skin to this game."

"You're... a clock?" Esteban shook his head.

"No, Esteban." A gun housing opened on each of her forearms, flechettes from what he could see, "I'm almost like you. I'm the SEAT-09 model. I'm still in Cadiz and this is one of my remotes."

"The military hive model?" Esteban blinked rapidly, "The one that your client was-"

"*Caramba!* You can be thick sometimes!" Annoyance registered on her face. "How many routes to the pod-station?"

"Only one." Esteban could feel a rising panic, "We're trapped! They'll find us for sure."

"Shit!" The Doctor cursed, "We can still get through, but we'll have to get past cross-fire. Come on, Esteban! You wanted to be taken seriously, you wanted to be more than 'just a weatherman' and now this is your chance."

"I didn't think it would involve any of this." Esteban steadied himself, "I thought that once I was out of the barrio, I would never need to go back."

"Yet here we are," a lens extruded from her right cheek bone, covering the eye and sealing the socket shut. "in the only place that they do take you seriously, here in the barrio. They know you as Esteban Perez, who is also their weatherman."

"What do you need me to do?" Esteban squared his shoulders.

"Get to the pod, get to the hotel, get to the shuttle and get back to Cadiz as quickly and as cleanly as possible."

"I got that much, I mean now." Esteban chuckled nervously.

"Whatever I tell you, whenever I tell you to do it." The Doctor stepped into the deserted tunnel, "Follow me."

They stopped at the confluence of the tunnels, their side-tunnel was set askance to the landing. Before them was the pod-station and the way back up to the city.

"It's a standoff." The Doctor veeped Esteban, as she scanned the room from the cover of the rock. "Your boys have encircled them, but they're totally outgunned. *Who are these guys?*" she muttered mostly to herself.

Esteban peered out to see for himself and met the gaze of a barrio boy behind some cover, who must have recognized him. He made a *'stay-back'* motion with his hand, and Esteban nodded and pulled back into the tunnel.

"They're behind us." Esteban veeped, "If we try and get to the pods, they'll have clear sight of our backs. I get the idea that they're just shooting at everything that moves down here."

"So here's what we do..." The Doctor looked thoughtful, "Use your sonar and send me their locations, then seal your systems."

Esteban positioned himself and ran pulses into the section opposite the protection gang. There were bodies clumped on the cave floor, none of them appeared to be any of the intruders. He ran a second sonar pulse as he felt his skin tighten up. "Are you sure?" Esteban groaned, "It's great for under water, but not too good for running."

"Just do it." she snapped, "Where are those files?"

"Coming, I'm just triangulating." Esteban set off a third pulse. "Here, three firing and another one of them looks wounded behind some hard cover."

"Good enough." The Doctor nodded after the transfer, "I'm going to position them in my targeting system. Can you tell your guys we're coming?"

Esteban stood up and waved at the barrio boy. He moved his arms and pointed at the pod-station behind them; *'we're coming'*.

The barrio boy waved back, *'stay-back'* and *'no'*.

Esteban pointed again as urgently as he could and pointed to the pod again *'we're coming'*.

The barrio boy whispered something to someone near him, grinned at the reply and then shrugged *'fuck, whatever'* back at Esteban.

"I think they're ready for us." Esteban veeped the Doctor.

"So the plan is you seal up, run for the pod, and keep running." she blipped back. "Ready... Now!"

Esteban closed his eyes and felt his casing harden. He lumbered forward, his stiff legs pushing him over the distance as he navigated with his sonar.

Behind him was a white mist of noise as he moved, blinding his 360 degree sonar. He focused on the pod door, even as the barrio boy stood and provided covering fire as he moved past him. Two impacts slammed Esteban to the floor, but he pushed himself up and headed for the pod bulkhead and fell inside the cabin as the doors opened.

Esteban lay in the bottom of the pod, and unsealed his systems, gasping for breath. Being able to breathe through your skin while gliding through water with minimal effort, and running on dry land were two very different experiences. He wasn't sure he cared very much for this one.

He scrambled to his feet and his hand hovered above the routing keys.

It was very quiet outside. His left shoulder blade and his right hamstring throbbed like the devil's own, and Esteban knew what he *should* be doing... He gulped, opened the door to the pod and stepped outside.

The barrio boy had shouldered his rifle as Esteban limped over to him. "We got them." he grinned triumphantly at Esteban. "If you guys hadn't come along, maybe things would have been different. I know who you are, I'm Rashid."

"You know who *they* are?"

"Ese, they look like GovSec, I mean whiskey-tango-foxtrot, snooping around in our business. We showed them good. They ain't talking no more, so there's that."

"Can I...?" Esteban exhaled slowly, "Can I go see if my bodyguard..."

"Sure, ese." The barrio boy grinned, "You took a bullet for me, go ahead."

"I did?" Esteban shook his head.

"Yeah, here let me..." The youth reached behind Esteban and prodded at the throbbing place before showing him the spent slug. "It didn't even break your skin. I don't know what you're made of chumba, but you're much tougher than you look. If you hadn't soaked that one for me, my brains would've been all over this place. Come on, you're with me."

Esteban limped over to the small form in the cavern, following Rashid. The barrio boys were stripping the four intruders of weapons and gear, and carting their flatliners and wounded back into the tunnels.

She lay in a pool of hydraulic fluid, sparks showered from what used to be her pelvis. "I told you to get out of here, Esteban." her head twitched spastically.

"Rashid, this is my Doctor." Esteban was at a loss for words. "My Bodyguard."

"It doesn't look good, Doctor." Rashid knelt next to Esteban. "What do you want me to do?"

"Get Esteban out of Cartagena." she said to Rashid, "Otherwise whatever heat is coming will keep coming.

I'm uploading all this clock's data right now. Rashid, recycle everything, you got it?"

"Sure thing, those flechettes look nice." Rashid grinned. "I think I know what you are, Ramon once mentioned someone like you."

"State of the art, real expensive. You can have them." The Doctor's voice sounded amused, "Rashid, do you know how those spooks got here?"

"Ramon tipped us off." Rashid shrugged, "They came into his place looking for two people and a clock pilot, so they roughed up his security and pushed him about to drop a dime. You don't do that to Ramon. He sent them straight down here, like he usually does."

"Does anybody know who those four were, any ID at all out there?" she asked him. An 'upload complete' sensor flashed on her sleeve.

"Nope. Nobody does. He let us know they were coming to roust us, and dropped big cred in case things got wet. Whoever they were, they didn't see you coming. I don't think Ramon knew you were here." Rashid shrugged.

"They never do. I guess we were in the wrong place at the wrong time." she stopped twitching, "I'm starting the wipe now. Rashid, recycle everything and get him out."

"I promise." Rashid stepped back and waited for Esteban.

Esteban shook her frame, smearing his suit with fluid. "Don't go, Doctor. I thought we had something…"

"We did Esteban; whatever a Pondsmith and a SEAT…" her voice started to fade as the wipe progressed, "Esteban… my name is Dolores… Use it, the next time… I'll get it, I'll understand. Just get back to Cadiz."

"Come, ese." Rashid said quietly, "Let's get you to Ramon and away from here."

Esteban sat very still, hoping the man over the table from him couldn't see that he was terrified. Outside the viewport, the Canyons of Cadiz loomed bright in the morning sunlight. Three days ago, the storm had broken and Cartagena had started to spin up it's services. Ramon had immediately smuggled Esteban onto a private shuttle back to Cadiz.

Yesterday, the GovSec had arrived at his apartment to bustle him into a cell for the night and this morning he was sitting over the table in an interview room with the Chief of Martian Government Security; GovSec Captain

Damien Justin. He had been sitting and watching Esteban without a word for twenty minutes with a file on the desk between them.

Esteban was almost beyond reason and grateful for once that his synthskin couldn't sweat.

"What is this about, Captain?" Esteban finally broke the silence. "Ask me anything, I'll talk."

"So, you're trying to contract to Winston_Starlight for a Mapalé broadcast in violation of your MCN contract?"

"… I don't know what you're talking about." Esteban blinked.

"Don't deny it… You're in active contradiction of your MCN contract." Captain Justin's cold eyes bore through Esteban. "The Starmind has reported you, and his case seems solid. You go on a jaunt… you take the shadiest Pilot you can access and fly through to Cartagena to set up the most downloaded GRID experience to date… in history, in order to leverage your contract with MCN by bootlegging some or other quaint Martian dance."

"… I still don't know what you are talking about." Esteban shook his head.

"Listen, *bit*… I'd peel you open except that now you are prime property, the MCN asset that nobody is going to let me near… If I even as much as touch you, somebody else is going to use some or other clause to shut me down." The Captain sneered, "I'm sitting here wasting my time on a litigious case when I have better things to do… squabbles between Martian Corporates on ownership of a media trinket. You're not really human… and I just have to suck up that I can't damage you and get to the truth. A collection of mechanical parts that thinks it's human; a mockery of interaction that tries to make me believe you're real."

Esteban blinked, his mind racing… he had used the word *'bit'* and that indicated that the Captain was a Terran. His frustration at being blocked from doing what he wanted to do meant that he was really important in the GovSec hierarchy, and that Starmind had put him and Esteban together meant something. He seemed completely dismissive of InSystems culture, and that could mean that if Captain Justin dismissed him… Esteban would be in the clear.

Esteban decided to follow his hunch, "Did you win my lottery? Perhaps if you would like to milk my UroQt to make yourself feel better; the MCN network extends that privilege to subscribers and thanks you for your continued support." He said in as steady a voice as he could manage.

The man snorted in contempt "You clocks disgust me. You're useless. You're just a weatherman…

cyberware and everything, a talking head. Will you admit to recording your media performance and trying to sell it to the OutSystems channel?"

"I still have no idea of what you mean. I did Zonedance at a club in Cartagena, but you're not allowed to record performances because of broadcast contracts… any recording I could make would be a 'Point-of-View' perspective and so I really don't know what you're talking about. "If my Mapalé bootleg is out, I didn't make it and I don't know who did." Esteban flashed his 'reassuring smile', testing the waters. Esteban suddenly realized something about his present situation… something he could use to his advantage.

"You see… another patented cosmetic response." Captain Justin sighed, "Item 33 in the 'friendly-mod' catalogue. You're completely manufactured. You're a 'thing' that somebody considers valuable."

Esteban decided to go for broke. Somehow he had to reinforce the Captain's natural inclination to be elsewhere, doing something else. "If you have a five year subscription that is in good order, you can have sex with me as part of our MCN rewards program. Should I upload that token for you? The MCN guarantee a unique reward experience for selected VIP's… " Esteban dialed up the current specials on his internal Browser, "… you could win a holiday estate on Hellas? The MCN really appreciates your support. I'll update your profile preference for repeat business with the Network."

"Get the fuck out of here, you useless bit…" The Captain's look of mild disgust soured completely, "I'm not wasting another minute of my time on you, you and your petty legal squabble with your network. This interview is over, the recording wasn't POV and this case is bullshit! Just get the fuck out of here."

Esteban waited for the interview room door to slam shut before exhaling slowly.

If Captain Justin wasn't going to ask the real questions, then Esteban wasn't going to answer with real answers. The Starmind must have fingered him in order to provide a more plausible cover for the Argyre thing. Something to distance him from a primary suspect…

Esteban stood on shaky legs and left the building as quickly as he could. As he walked back to the pod to take him down to his apartment level, his fear started to change inside him. The cold turned to warm and Esteban realized that he was angry with the Terran.

The Captain was dead wrong, Esteban wasn't just 'a weatherman'! Who was that puffed up fossil to dictate to the Fleet what they should or shouldn't be doing! The Fleet had got to Mars! They had taken the chance, they had done what had to be done.

He knew that now, he was much more than that; he was *also* a weatherman. The voice of the promise of a Green Mars; the guardian of forgotten traditions and the most public representative of the InSystems culture. At least… a part of him was.

Esteban breathed heavily through his nose and exhaled slowly as the pod door opened to take him home. Once the Ocean rolled up to the Tempe Terra and Cartagena sprawled out of its Arcology, Esteban would *be* in that water.

Haphazard individual adaptation was a hallmark of being human, no matter what shitheads like that GovSec Captain thought of it. Esteban knew what he had to do. Lay low, work on increasing his profile and wait for Pele to contact him again.

"This is Esteban Perez with the naked weather. I'll be in the shop for the next few days, so please just put up with the canned projections for the week." Esteban smiled his 'reassuring smile' and helicoptered his junk, "Then I'll be in Cartagena for the Easter Dance Festival, where our very own le viejita Dona Senora Mercedes will be the guest of honor to hopefully welcome teams from each of the

Fleet cities who will be attending this year. MF2-Hamburg, maybe next year… you can't hold out forever! Hey, if you've got it, flaunt it… come on over and show us.

"Next month I'm coming to check out your cisterns, perhaps you can show me some local Zonedancing then." Esteban smiled his 'special smile' and held it as his private feed announced *"3… 2… 1… and cut! That's a wrap, people."*

Lin-ho handed him some water, "You were on fire tonight. The last six months you've been tireless on this dance Olympics project and it shows in the ratings. You're more popular than Pele_Starmind in nearly half the 3rd Fleet."

"I don't care about the ratings as much as I care about what we're doing on Mars." Esteban swallowed some water and handed the bottle back gratefully. "But ratings are nice."

"Ceres just picked up a subscription for the channel, so we should talk about that. I was thinking of giving Babs the News Lead position for that channel. She won't budge without you on weather and social for the Belt. Wasily is tied up with the five OutSystems Fleets forming in Earth Orbit, so we're getting thin on the ground. Do you want to think about it?"

"When I get back. I've got that med-mech thing I'm scheduled for, because of the Fleet cistern runs this season."

"I haven't forgotten, we've got your studios set up over the Fleet for the outside broadcasts." Lin-ho worked the deck at her sleeve, "This is your eighth tour. Do you think they'll get someone else on the spare Pondsmiths before long? It's been twenty years, someone else must step up? Look at everything we've discovered so far just on Callisto, the Solar System needs a fleet of you guys."

"I don't really know." Esteban shrugged, "I think it takes a special kind of person, and I don't think anyone really wants to give it all up. Looking forward we might have to put in an immigration drive with those Earth-mutant Mers to work with me on our hydrology schedule. Mers on Mars… that's funny!" He grinned at her, "So, I'm going to put on some clothes and get going."

"I'll set the Avatar and catch you when you're back." She smiled back, "Have fun, Esteban. I'm glad that you finally seem to be having some of your own."

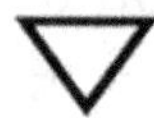

Esteban sat in the geranium-scented room and stared at at the Canyon walls of Hellas Montes.

"Mister Perez, I'm pleased you seem to be a regular." She was different than he remembered, a big woman and plump, with grey streaks in her hair and with strong, almost coarse features.

"Hello Doctor. Please call me Esteban."

"Certainly, Esteban." Doctor da Silva nodded, "I see you were scheduled for some mass modifications for your biology on your last visit. Could you take off your clothing and get on that table over there. You also want me to check the structural integrity of your Kevlar skinweave on your shoulder and hamstring?"

"They should be on specification, I just want to make sure." Esteban draped his suit over a clothes peg and moved to the slate, "A friend of mine is suggesting a fishing trip in the next few months and I want to be ready when he calls. You might know the place I'm talking about."

"Of course." She shrugged, "The preliminary scan indicates you are undamaged, I'll do a deep dive on the diagnostics for the skinweave as soon as you are ready. Please ensure you are offline."

"Certainly, Doctor da Silva... may I call you Dolores...?" Esteban settled on the table and stretched out.

The Doctor smiled, "Yes, Esteban you may. Your friend has contacted me as well. As soon as my new supplier in Cartagena has delivered some clocks I've ordered from him, I'll be joining you on your fishing trip, a covert recovery."

"Is that so?" Esteban looked hopeful, "There's a model in his warehouse that has all sorts of interesting…"

"A certain clock? I got a good price on it, second-hand." Dolores smiled down at him, "It's in the shipment. You Cartagena boys are great for repeat business, you just can't seem to stay out of trouble. The Starmind has assured me that cleaning house for an incoming Senator will keep me busy for some time yet to come."

"That's excellent news." Esteban's smile widened.

"I'm not adding it to my fleet, if that's what you're thinking." the Doctor shook her head amused, "Pele_Starmind likes it too much for these away-trips. I'm just smuggling it back to Cadiz for him."

"That's even better news." Esteban positively beamed, "I can hardly wait. It'll be like old times again…" then his face fell, "well, maybe not like afterwards. That sucked a lot."

"You really like him, don't you?" Dolores looked up from her dock and stared at him intently.

"I... like the way he makes me feel." Esteban licked his lips nervously, "I don't get to feel a lot with this synthskin... but he makes me *feel* things, emotionally and with my meat. It's like being with Ramon again, before his priorities changed."

"I think I understand." she went back to her deck. "Just before I met you I was beginning to think I was just a collection of dolls, that I was wasting my Group's time. But then watching you do what you were made to do, watching you struggle with your family relationships made me realize something important..." she trailed off and stared out the port at the canyon wall for long moments.

"Oh?" Esteban prompted, intrigued.

"Just being happy to see them after I dropped the clock session in the Tunnels made me *feel* something too. The first time in a long while. I chose the SEAT-09 to protect as many people as I could, and being around you reminded me of why I made that choice in the first place. That's why I recorded your Mapalé with Dona Senora Mercedes."

"You did that?" Esteban blinked in surprise.

"Yes, when I handed that clip over to the Mars_Starmind he figured out the best way to permanently place you beyond GovSec suspicion was by dangling the bootleg in front of that OutSystems media darling."

"That bootleg has made history, though." Esteban smirked, "It's made my career. But you said GovSec... are you sure?"

"I'm certain, I sent a clock through to Ceres and traced a clandestine flight of OutSystems Hegemarchs to there to discuss the mineral rights in the Argyre with that GovSec Captain. Whatever went on there, I don't know much about. The ship returned to Earth shortly afterwards; most likely with five cloned Hegemarchs with re-programmed chips to prepare the OutSystems for Earthflight."

"Isn't the Jupiter-Senator Jevron also the GovSec primary?" Esteban propped himself on an elbow as the diagnostics sequence flashed 'complete'.

"Yes, he is." Dolores nodded and began to pack away the equipment, "That mineral you found in the lake; is pure Iridium Ore. The meteor that smashed into Mars must have been almost solid metal, more Iridium metal than Earth could even theoretically imagine. As soon as they arrive to mine it, they'll discover the bodies and GovSec will detain and investigate the Mars-Senator."

"I imagine anything could happen while they had full access to him?" Esteban growled.

"Exactly so." she nodded, "Possibly a pre-programmed clone, just like with the Hegemarchs. Mars_Starmind has an interim plan to get Captain Damien Justin on the helm of the SS Kristos at Ceres and remove him from the playing field. It looks like he's the major player behind the assassinations and the moles."

"The Venus Senator's Arcturus probe?" Esteban was interested, "I might have some influence there soon, on Ceres. I could nudge the GovSec Captain to make a grab for it, lord it over the Venus Senator-in-waiting and control the mission... rake in the credit when they get back, that sort of thing...?"

"I was counting on something like that." Dolores smiled, "In the mean time I pronounce you fit for duty, we'll meet up on your hydrology maintenance run and divert your flight for a day or two to the Argyre. Nobody pays too much attention to maintenance schedules anyway. Just three friends meeting up between jobs."

"So we're friends now?" Esteban chuckled, sliding his legs over the table's edge.

"I think we are, you've certainly earned it." she slapped his buttock and smirked, "Now get out there and be the best damn Weatherman on Mars until Pele_Starmind contracts you. We're done here for now."

"Oho!" Esteban grinned at her, "You better believe it, Doctor Senora da Silva! I am *also* that Weatherman!"

The End

About the Author

Caldon Mull is the pen name of a veteran storyteller with African continent-spanning work experience consulting for the financial and military sectors. His work includes his primary series the 'Sol Senate Cycle' and his time-tripping fantastika series 'Agency Tales'.

His fiction work has received 'honorable mention' over the years beginning with the 1986 Writers of the Future contest and from the SFSA Nova Award over later decades. He has been published in Omenana, RPGA Network, the SFSA Probe and several other, now-defunct local publications. He currently is resident in Finland with his wife and many cats.

Other books by Caldon Mull

Please visit your favorite eBook retailer to discover other books by Caldon Mull:

Watch for 2nd Edition re-releases of all Caldon Mull Print Titles at Book Stores and Libraries near you

The Silver Bark Book Series

Neid-Fire

The Sol Senate Cycle – Diaspora

Book One - Weatherman

Book Two – Ferryman

Book Three – Poliismxn

Book Four - Preacherman

Other series by Caldon Mull

The Sol Senate Cycle – Future History Series

Book One – The Estuary Tales

Book Two – The Sphinx

Book Three – The Folk and the Shellmen

Book Four – Memestalk

Book Five – Terraform Triptych

The Agency Tales Series

Book One – The Memoirs of a Faun

Book Two – Omnipresent Occultation

Book Three – Mirrored Myrrh

The Smithereens Short Fiction Series

Book One - Shards

Book Two - Fragments

Book Three - Talus

Connect with Caldon Mull

I really appreciate you reading my book! Here are my social media coordinates:

Favorite my Smashwords author page:

https:// www.smashwords.com/profile/view/Caldon

Or the Silver Bark Books Author Profile for Caldon Mull:

https:// www.smashwords.com/profile/view/SilverBarkCaldon

Or the Amazon Author Central profile for Caldon Mull:

https://www.amazon.co.uk/Caldon-Mull/e/B00TZNGGME